HELL HOUSE
XXX
(PART 1)

WOL-VRIEY

Burning Bulb
PUBLISHING

HELL HOUSE
XXX
(PART 1)

WOL-VRIEY

Burning Bulb
PUBLISHING

Hell House XXX (Part 1)
By **Wol-vriey**

Burning Bulb Publishing
P.O. Box 4721
Bridgeport, WV 26330-4721
United States of America
www.BurningBulbPublishing.com

Cover designed by Gary Lee Vincent.

First Edition.

Paperback Edition ISBN: 978-1-964172-37-8

CHAPTER 1

Paul & Marko

"I don't believe in ghosts," Paul Dunford told the dark heavyset man seated opposite him.

The man was his brother-in-law, Boston crime kingpin Marko Velli.

"I know you don't believe in spooks," Marko Velli replied him. "That's why you're perfect for this job."

Paul's response to Marko's statement was to nod his head slowly in a noncommittal way. He was still confused by this urgent summons to Marko's presence this morning.

"You simply want me to housesit some supposedly haunted house in Raynham over the weekend?"

Marko nodded. "Yup, that's all, Paul."

Were it not for the completely unamused look on the crime lord's face, Paul might have imagined Marko was having him on. But Marko's dark eyes were as cold as ever, wet ball bearings that reflected the gears of the man's criminal mind.

It was 10 o'clock on Friday morning. The two men were seated in Marko Velli's office, up on the tenth floor of the Boston waterfront building that he owned.

The weather was cold and Paul was shivering a little now. For some reason, the heater in the office wasn't working. Paul would have loved a cup of coffee to warm him up, but Marko hadn't offered him one. He thought of asking for coffee, but then thought better of it.

Here the guy is, talking about ghosts. There's no telling how erratic he'll get if I prompt him in the wrong direction.

Paul took a moment to stare out of the windows of his brother-in-law's office.

Marko Velli said he liked working up this high because it gave him a great view of Boston Harbor. His enemies claimed he liked his windows facing the ocean because snipers couldn't target him from that direction. Not entirely true though, as Marko had once been shot

1

at from an incoming helicopter. As a result, his office windows were now made of bulletproof glass.

"Can I at least have a little more info before I say yes to this?" Paul asked, in that same noncommittal tone, although it wasn't like he had any real choice in the matter.

Nope, I've had no damn choice in the matter since I got that phone call from Marko two hours ago, insisting I be here promptly at ten. Marko's already made up his mind as to what he wants me to do; this conversation is merely a formality.

He frowned and tapped his fingers on his side of Marko's desk.

"What's all this really about?" he asked Marko. "What's really going on here?"

Marko frowned back at him and suddenly looked angry. Then, after staring at Paul for a while as if Paul was to blame for whatever was the problem, he said: "You're part of the family, man, so I'll level with you on this. This crap all began about a month ago, when I decided to buy my mama a new house . . ."

Paul nodded.

"Well, so my people looked around a bit," Marko continued, "until they finally found this sweet little place down in Raynham."

"Why Raynham?" Paul asked.

Marko smiled a tight smile. "Well, 'cos I needed somewhere a bit out of the way, but not too far from Boston, so I can still visit mama on the weekends."

Paul nodded. "This all has got to do with my sis and your mom not getting along, don't it?"

Marko grimaced, but shook his head emphatically. "No, no, it ain't that. My wife . . . your older sister Petra . . . shit, who'd ever have imagined that after fifteen years of knowing each other, those two still wouldn't have arrived at some kind of relationship that didn't involve yelling around the house?" Then he sighed and looked sad. "No, what's going on is that mama's getting soft in the head now."

He looked straight at Paul while saying this last, and for those brief moments Paul almost felt like Marko Velli, who was one of America's most feared and ruthless criminals, had a soul, a normal empathic human soul like everyone else.

But then either that moment of revelation passed, or Paul himself popped the balloon of his self-delusion.

2

"Okay, so why not put her in a nursing home?" Paul asked. Paul was surprised to hear that the old woman's mind was going. Unlike her only son, Danika Velli was a nice person.

She seemed alright last time I was up at Marko's place. Okay, that was five months ago on Petra's birthday. I guess five months is more than enough time for mental rot to set in, or at least become apparent.

Marko shook his head. "Nah, nah, dude. I don't want my mom at the mercy of some mean nurses who'll treat her like shit. I want a place of her own for her. Somewhere where I'll be the one hiring the staff to look after her, so I know she's being well taken care of."

"But why not up in Boston?"

"Paul, just shut up and listen, okay. This is simply the background. You're getting these details 'cos you're Petra's younger brother and I don't want you havin' the wrong idea 'bout what's happening."

Paul nodded. "I'm listening."

Marko nodded back at him. "Yeah, just listen." Then he seemed to remember something and frowned. "Hey, we don't have any coffee in here. Why the fuck don't we have any coffee?"

Before Paul could either comment or not on this, Marko stabbed the intercom button on his desk.

"Yes, sir?" a pleasant female voice asked.

"We need coffee, Therese. Hurry it up, girl, I can feel my balls freezing."

"At once, sir."

Once the intercom disconnected, Marko returned his attention to Paul, who was relieved that he'd soon feel warmer.

"So, to get back to what we're talking about, a month ago, my guys found my mama this cute house in Raynham. We both saw the pictures of the place and she liked it and the price was right, and so I got Tommy Burke to liquify the funds for the purchase."

Paul now raised a finger like he was in class. "Hey, I heard that Tommy Burke's dead."

Marko nodded. "Yeah, he is. He got murdered right after sending the funds for the house. That very same night."

Paul was about to comment on this, but Marko raised a finger of his own. "No. Don't you ask no questions 'bout Tommy. Keep listening to me. So, Tommy sends me the funds I need and I pay for the house, which was going cheap—the previous owner has apparently been dead for years and years and no one else wanted to own the place. Anyhow, long story short, I buy the house, get it cleaned up and furnished, and then load mama in my car to go visit her new residence."

Marko stopped talking. Paul wasn't certain if this was because he wanted to emphasize his point, or because the memory hurt him, or because right at that point the door to his office opened and his secretary Therese walked in.

Paul nodded politely to Therese as she served them their coffee and a tray of cookies. He appreciated the cookies as he'd not yet had breakfast. He ate a cookie, drank some coffee, and immediately felt a lot better.

"Will that be all, sir?" Therese asked Marko.

He waved her away and she departed.

Marko took a sip of his own coffee, ate part of a cookie, and then went on with his tale:

"Anyhow, Paulie, we arrive at mama's new house, she takes one look at the damn place and refuses to get out of the fucking car."

Before he heard this, Paul had been about sipping some more coffee, but the statement surprised him so much that he paused with the hot mug pressed against his lips, which resulted in him scalding his tongue.

Scowling from the pain, he carefully put down the mug and stared at Marko. "She refused to leave the car? Why?"

Marko laughed coldly. "Mama told me in no uncertain terms that the new house I'd just bought for her was haunted."

Paul laughed too, but in amusement. "Haunted. But, you just said . . . she's going a bit . . ." he twisted his right index finger near his right temple. "Couldn't it just be old age?"

Marko shook his head. "I'd love to think that was the case. I tried everything I could—short of physically lifting her out of the car—to make her get out of it and enter the damn building, but she flat-out refused to budge. And so in the end, we turned the car around and drove back here." He laughed again, a more humorous sound this time. "Actually, mama doesn't just claim the house is haunted, she claims it's cursed. Cursed by the devil. She called the place 'Hell House.'"

In the interim Paul had managed to drink some more coffee. "How the hell did she come to that conclusion? I mean without setting foot inside of the place?"

4

Marko shook his head again. "She's always been superstitious like that. Right from when we both lived in Europe. Back in the old country, mama regularly visited mediums and psychics. She kept up those practices here too."

The 'old country' was Croatia, from where Marko had emigrated two-and-a-half decades ago.

"Okay, I think I understand this better," Paul said. "So, to prove to mama that she's wrong, you need someone to live in the house for a few days?"

Marko nodded and smiled. "And I thought to myself, who better to offer this housesitting job to than my good friend and brother-in-law Paulie, who just also happens to owe me a hundred-and-fifty grand?"

Paul winced at the reminder.

Paul Dunford knew very well that the sole reason he wasn't yet dead, the only reason that he wasn't yet buried somewhere out in the Atlantic Ocean, was because he was Marko's brother-in-law.

Marko Velli had burnt men to death for much less money—as little as a $5,000 loan default, in fact.

However, Marko might have been many things—ruthless, brutal, and downright sick in the head at times—but one thing he could never be faulted on was his dedication to family.

Where Marko was concerned, family came first.

No—family came second . . . after money. But family still rated very highly with him.

And so, 38-year-old Paul Dunford, who'd borrowed $150,000 from Marko to help finance a dry-cleaning business that unfortunately never took off, continued to breathe the cool clean air of God's green earth, while lesser men ('lesser' in terms of the amount of money that they'd borrowed from Marko) had already departed God's green earth to meet Him in person.

"Hey, I'll make you a deal on this," Marko said. "You stay in the house over this weekend and I'll write off your entire debt."

"Huh?" Paul was so shocked by Marko's offer of debt cancellation that he spilled what remained of his coffee over his pants. Thankfully, there was very little left in the mug and that little amount was now tepid, and his pants were dark colored, but that didn't stop Marko from scowling at him.

"Hey, dumbass, watch that you don't ruin the rug—it's fucking *expensive*," Marko coldly told him. "I'm trying to clear one debt here. Don't be so dumb as to create another one for yourself that I ain't gonna forgive."

"I'll try to be more careful," Paul sputtered back at him. "But . . . but, are you serious about clearing my debts if I do this?"

Marko smiled. "Yeah, I am. Way I got this figured out, you can't afford to pay me anyhow—you got no head for business, and you ain't got the nerve to get your hands dirty with mob work; risky stuff like running drugs or guns for me. You won't even make a good pimp: if I put you in charge of my working girls, they'll walk all over you. And . . . and I also realize that Petra won't ever let me waste you, so this is a win-win situation for us both: You perform this small job for me—convince mama that her new home ain't haunted . . . or convince me that it is . . . and we're straight. You won't owe me nada, and I won't be upset and frustrated that I can't have you killed and incinerated." Marko scowled. "Just don't fucking ask me to loan you any more money and you'll be sure to live to a grand old age."

Paul began trembling again.

Killed and incinerated? Marko is discussing my possible exit from life the way one discusses squashing roaches; like it's something of no consequence.

"Okay, I'll do it," he said.

Marko laughed and got up from his desk. "I knew you would," he said, while brushing cookie crumbs off his pants.

He stepped around to the front of the desk and sat on the edge close to Paul.

Being this near to Marko disconcerted Paul. He was very well aware that this man beside him reeked of blood.

Not literally, of course, but Marko Velli has enough blood on his hands to make even the devil envious.

Marko squinted at Paul.

"Hey, you sure you're okay? I know you've always been pale, but today you look almost as white as Caspar."

Hearing this, Paul studied the pink backs of his hands. They seemed normal enough to him, though his brother-in-law was right: he really did need to find a beach somewhere to work on his tan. He made a fist of his right hand and studied the short brown hairs between his knuckles with calm brown eyes.

"I'm fine," he replied Marko after this appraisal. "Never felt better."

"That's great." Marko laughed. "I don't want you staring at your own reflection in one of the mirrors over there and imagining that you're a ghost."

I don't believe in ghosts, Paul thought doggedly, finally grabbing up another of the cookies, which he'd more-or-less forgotten about since Marko had mentioned wiping his slate clean.

"I don't believe in ghosts," Paul once again told Marko, after biting into the cookie, feeling that he had to make some kind of a point.

Marko Velli grinned back at him. "I know, I once heard you arguing with your sister 'bout that. That's why you're the best guy I know for the job. Other folks, myself included, are either downright superstitious or are susceptible to being fooled by our emotions into seeing stuff that ain't there." He gestured outward with his hands. "The door bangs upstairs or the basement squeaks as the house settles and tra la la, we all immediately remember some paranormal psychic TV show that we've watched and assume there's spooks in the building. With you, I don't got that problem. You're skeptical, so you're not gonna report ghosts except they actually exist."

"Okay, just so that I understand this correctly: how many days do I have to stay at this so called 'Hell House' of yours?"

Marko scratched his chin. "Just this single weekend. Tonight, tomorrow night, and Sunday night too."

"Marko, I've gotta be at work on Monday morning. They're already gonna be pissed off at the way I begged off this morning."

Paul had a temporary job working at the dockyards. He'd originally been in his brother-in-law's employ, but since he'd lost the money that Marko had loaned him, Marko refused to employ him anymore.

Marko's lips turned down and his eyes turned a shade colder as he leaned menacingly towards Paul. "No, you don't got to be at work on Monday morning, dumbass. And that's 'cos I'm paying you the sum of one-hundred-fifty grand—yeah, that hundred and fifty grand that you still owe me—to housesit for me for three days. That averages out to about 50,000 dollars a day. So, I don't wanna hear any crap about your bullshit fifteen-dollars-an-hour employment."

"Sure, sure," Paul quickly agreed.

Paul was relieved when Marko got to his feet and stomped his way back around to the far side of his desk. The man rummaged in the desk drawer for a few moments and then lobbed a set of keys across the table to Paul.

"The house keys," Marko explained after Paul snapped the keys out of the air. "Hey, don't lose 'em, 'cos the realtors say they can't locate the other sets."

"And the house address?"

"I'll text it to you. Now, get your ass home, get packed, and get down there." Marko rummaged in his desk drawer again and then flung a wad of money at Paul. "Use this for living expenses. I don't wanna hear no crap 'bout how you had to leave Raynham for a while 'cos you were broke." He raised an eyebrow. "Oh yeah, and take Jenny with you. Take your slacker friend Billy too, if he's free this weekend. In fact, the more the merrier: invite as many people down there as you can get. The more witnesses the better."

Paul nodded and pocketed the money. Then he got to his feet, shook hands with Marko, and left the man's office.

While descending in the elevator, he counted the cash Marko had given him. Two thousand dollars.

Paul whistled softly to himself.

Wow! Marko's giving me good money to housesit that place. This is really serious.

CHAPTER 2

Isadora & Joe

This wasn't the first time that Joe Parker had gotten violent with Isadora Grant, but from all current indications, it looked like it might be the last time.

For her, that was.

At the moment, Isadora was bleeding from a cut lip, had a black eye, and one of her ribs felt like it might be broken.

She was running through her house in downtown Raynham, MA in her nightgown, with Joe coming hard after her.

This Friday afternoon, Joe was as drunk as usual. Laid off from yet another job, Joe had been drowning his sorrows in liquor since sunup, until Isadora had either said or done something to set off the beast that lurked behind his bloodshot eyes.

In fact, the reason why Isadora had a black eye was because Joe had earlier hit her in the face with the whiskey bottle he was holding.

She counted herself lucky that the bottle hadn't shattered and filled her left eye with glass. And that he'd not gotten sufficient of a swing going with the bottle to knock her out with it.

She didn't feel lucky enough to hang around though.

And so, with Joe hard on her heels, she was running away for what her life was worth.

Isadora Grant realized that calling for help would be a waste of time.

Joe and I fight so much that our neighbors no longer call the cops during our domestics. Even the cops are tired of us.

She made it out into her living room and darted across the living room to the front door.

And then she discovered that the front door was locked. And that the keys weren't in the lock.

Where's the keys?

And then her violent boyfriend had a tight grip on her hair and was spinning her around to face him.

"You lookin' for these, bitch?"

9

On seeing the house keys in Joe's hand, Isadora felt angry.

"Give me the keys, asshole!" she spat defiantly at him.

His response was to punch her hard in the belly. She wheezed in pain and all of the air in her lungs felt static and frozen for a few moments. Then she exhaled and inhaled and tried to reason with Joe.

"You're gonna kill me!" she gasped.

He punched her again, this time catching her on the side of the jaw and knocking her down to the floor.

She sat against the wall in a crumpled mess. The latter punch had knocked all of the fight out of her. The pain in her gut made breathing difficult.

Joe squatted so that his face was level with hers.

"I've told you more than once that you can't ever leave me. You're *my* woman, and that's that. I'm not gonna stand for you cheating on me."

Isadora felt like she was swimming through the alcoholic ocean of Joe's breath.

"I'm *not* cheating on you, dickhead." Talking hurt. Joe seemed to have almost dislocated her lower jaw.

"That's not what I've been hearing. People have been seeing you with that black dyke Sharday."

"Sharday's my friend. We've been friends since high school; you know that. There's nothing going on between us. You know I love you."

Of recent, it was becoming easier for Isadora to lie like this. Why tell him the truth, that she hated his guts?

It already looks like I'm not gonna survive tonight; why help death kill me?

Joe tilted the whiskey bottle up and chugged down the last mouthful of brown liquor. With his other hand he reached out and grabbed a handful of Isadora's right breast and twisted it painfully.

She gasped, but not too loudly.

"Listen, bitch," Joe told her, his eyes red as coals and his breath so alcoholic that Isadora felt she was being anesthetized by it. "Listen here. I know you're screwing that black girlfriend of yours. I just haven't caught you two at it yet. But when I do . . ." For emphasis he made a fist of his left hand and waved it in Isadora's face, and then slapped her for good measure.

"Joe, I'm not sleeping with Sharday. It's all in your head," Isadora wheezed at him when her ears had stopped ringing from the slap.

My soul hurts and my body hurts too.

She now had the epiphany that Joe had progressively gotten 'better' at abusing her during their four years together. The grip he had on her breast felt like he'd located all of the acupuncture points in there and was giving them a workout.

They're right—practice really does make perfect.

A crazy thought maybe, but Isadora Grant wasn't exactly in a sane frame of mind. At the moment, her primary objective was survival. She had no chance in hell of beating Joe up. He was almost six foot tall, while she was a petite woman.

He threw the empty bottle away over his shoulder and then let go of her breast also.

Isadora's thoughts that she'd won a brief respite from the abuse vanished when next, Joe produced a switchblade knife from somewhere.

"Noooo!" she gasped as he flicked the blade out. "Don't!"

She attempted to get to her feet then, but he shoved her back down with his left hand.

Frightened of what Joe intended to do to her with the knife, Isadora continued fighting to get up and flee.

Her escape attempt ended when Joe punched her so hard in the gut that it felt like he'd just nailed her to the wall. She slumped back down in the angle between the wall and the floor and stared up at him in a delirium of agony.

She felt too far gone to even hate Joe.

I just gotta survive tonight. God, please, help me survive this sonofabitch tonight, and I'll leave him for good and never look back.

This of course, would be difficult, since she owned the house that they lived in. But maybe this time she'd succeed in getting a restraining order put on Joe.

Joe waved the knife in her face. That last drink of whiskey he'd had was clearly getting to him now. His grip on the knife was slack. And his eyes were unfocused. Saliva dribbled from the left edge of his mouth into his brown beard.

Isadora gasped in horror as Joe inched the blade of the knife closer and closer to her face. Soon the point of the switchblade was just a few centimeters from her right eye. She wanted to close her eyes to avoid looking at the approaching silver blade, but didn't dare to.

"No, baby, don't hurt me!" she gasped at him. "Please, don't."

Her plea amused him and he laughed at her, his breath almost making her throw up.

He placed the knife against the bridge of her nose and grinned at her. "This is the only warning I'm gonna give ya, bitch. If I so much as see you looking at Sharday again, I'm gonna slice your nose off. And then we'll see how your lezzie friend likes you then."

The feel of the cold steel blade pressed against her nose made Isadora shiver. She knew that Joe wasn't kidding. Normally, when he wasn't drunk, he wasn't violent with her, but those 'normal' periods were becoming less and less frequent.

"Do you understand me?" Joe asked her. When she didn't immediately reply him, he pulled the knife gently along her nose, drawing blood. "I'm gonna cut your damn nose off!"

She winced as the red flow trickled down her face. "Okay, okay. I won't talk to Sharday again!"

Joe relaxed a little. "Not ever? I mean, I love you, girl, but I ain't sharing you with no dyke. I'd rather kill you than let that woman steal you from me."

The blood streaming from the cut on Isadora's nose had now met with that from her split lip. She licked the blood away and then weakly wagged her head at her raging boyfriend. "Yeah, not ever, Joey honey. I promise not to ever even *talk* to Sharday again . . . in my life."

Anything, anything to survive tonight. And then we're so through that we could be a tunnel, asshole!

She sighed with relief when he pulled the knife away from her face.

But strangely, even though he had backed off, Isadora felt like the danger wasn't yet over. Because, Joe looked uncertain.

To her mind, Joe looked like he felt she deserved more punishment.

Hell no! Isadora thought. *You're not beating me again!*

At that moment, Isadora Grant felt as if her life hung in the balance, her living or dying to be decided by the motion of fate's pendulum. And she had no idea which way that pendulum would swing.

Isadora had never considered herself to be one of life's great fighters. But she didn't want to die when she was just thirty years old.

So, because Isadora felt that Joe might still attack her with the knife if he felt jealous enough, she decided to attack him first.

"You know . . ." Joe began telling her, but then he paused and glanced aside at the kitchen door.

Taking advantage of Joe's distraction, Isadora flung herself at him and headbutted him hard in the face.

Joe went over backwards and lay panting on the floor.

Isadora thought she'd broken his nose. Blood streamed from it and each time he breathed out, he snorted crimson drops up at her face.

Isadora grinned at the red mess she'd made of Joe's face. And then, energized by her success at knocking him down, she hastily looked around for his knife.

Damn! Joe's still holding on to the knife!

Still, Isadora made a grab for it. For a few moments, boyfriend and girlfriend fought silently for possession of the weapon.

Joe finally won their contest, but only after the blade had gashed his palm open.

Joe stood there, with blood dripping both from his now lopsided nose and from his wounded hand. The blood from his nose was dribbling down over his lips and his chin.

Except for the fact that they couldn't see their own faces, they could be reflections of similar brutal usage.

To Isadora, Joe looked crazy. Crazy enough to murder her.

Shit! Now I've really gone and done it.

"Please don't kill me, baby!" she pleaded, once more on the defensive when he took a step towards her.

She backed away from Joe's approach until her back met the wall.

Joe looked down at his bleeding hand, and then up at her again.

"You're so fucking useless, I *should* kill ya . . . but ya ain't worth going to jail for," he told Isadora.

Then he threw the knife away across the living room.

"I didn't mean to cut you, baby," she began pleading, not pointing out the obvious: that she was bleeding too and it was all his doing, all the result of tonight's abuse. "Honest. It was an acci—"

"Shut up!" Joe interrupted her.

Isadora saw the punch he'd flung at her coming through the air. Joe's bunched knuckles seemed to float towards her in slow-motion.

But there was nothing slow-mo about the way Joe's fist made contact with the side of her head. The punch totally rocked her mind. Its force flung her sideways and draped her across the living room couch.

She lay there like a broken doll with the lights in her brain switching off.

"Fuck, I need a drink," Isadora heard Joe say as she lost consciousness.

CHAPTER 3

Isadora

Isadora regained consciousness after only God-knew-how-long.

Her head rung like a bell and various parts of her body hurt like hell. It was with great effort that she managed to keep from passing out again.

It took Isadora a little time to both realize where she was—lying prone on the living room couch—and to remember why that was.

Once she'd remembered, Isadora looked around for danger. No, Joe wasn't in sight, though there had to be at least two six-packs of empty beer cans strewn across the coffee table and the living room rug. Meaning he was likely passed out drunk in their bedroom.

The pains in her body were brutal injections of memory. Her face hurt in multiple places, and her chest hurt and her belly hurt. Multiple agonies replayed multiple hits with her body as the drumkit.

Damn Joe! Well, I survived today's ordeal. And now we're officially through. No more pleas for forgiveness from him once he sobers up.

But then Isadora became aware of something odd.

I was lying on my back when I passed out. I'm certain I was. But now . . . now I'm lying on my belly.

And this was when Isadora became aware that her butt hurt, specifically her anus.

Oh, no, he didn't—Joe didn't rape my ass again while I was passed out!

This was easy to investigate. Isadora slipped a hand back between her buttocks and patted herself there. The pain she felt once she touched the entrance to her exit assured her that, yes, she had been anally violated when unconscious. The wetness she felt there assured her that her violent drunken boyfriend had ejaculated up her butt, and when she brought her hand back to her face and looked at it, she saw that Joe clearly hadn't been gentle about it either.

Her fingertips were red, crimson streaked with the occasional brown and whitish smear.

What the hell did Joe do to me down there?

Isadora's memory of the hard beating that she'd survived already had her enraged. But this proof of the mess that her abuser had made of her ass, boosted her anger up into the stratosphere.

Alright, that's IT! It's fucking O.V.E.R! Joe's abuse ends for good today!

She sat up on the couch, and then got to her feet. A perfunctory look out of the window revealed that the sun was low in the east sky. The clock by the TV gave the time as a quarter to six p.m.

That means I've been unconscious for three hours. And Joe didn't bother to call an ambulance for me. Sonofabitch!

Once sure that her legs were steady, Isadora staggered her slow and painful way out of the living room and down the hallway to she and Joe's bedroom.

As she'd anticipated, Joe was passed out in bed, snoring loudly.

She walked past him into the bathroom and got out some caplets of Tylenol from the bathroom cabinet. After swallowing those, she walked back out into the bedroom, picked up her handbag, and then returned to the living room.

Back in the living room, she got her cellphone out of her bag.

She opened up WhatsApp, located 'Sharday Brooks' in her chat list, and dialed up a videocall.

Isadora's placing a videocall was deliberate; she knew that once Sharday saw her battered face, she'd drop whatever she was doing and hurry over.

Today was Isadora's own day off work at Cashstretch and she knew that today Sharday had had the morning shift at the clinic where she worked. So, Sharday should be back home now. But there was always the possibility that she was busy, or was out with some girlfriends.

Isadora sat with grim expectation while the call connected.

Then Sharday Brooks' dusky face filled the phone screen. From the onscreen background, she seemed to be at home. No afterwork dates this Friday.

"Hey, girl, what's up?" Sharday asked. Then her eyes widened in horror. "What the hell happened to your face?"

"Girl, get your ass over here right now," Isadora said tight-lipped, unaware that squeezing up her lips like a prune before speaking had inadvertently reopened her cut lip and was making blood dribble down to her chin. "Tonight, we're taking out the trash."

She watched her words sink into her friend's mind.

"Did Joe do this to you?" Sharday asked, her look of horror now hardening and her lips tightening into an expression of hatred. "I'll murder him if he did this to you."

Isadora smiled coldly. "Come over right now. Don't allow me the time to change my mind."

Sharday considered her words for about a second, and then nodded. "What's the asshole doing now?"

"Passed out as expected. He ain't gonna wake up till morning."

"Alright, I'll be there in fifteen minutes. If you're planning on doing what I think you are, we're gonna need some stuff."

Isadora Grant nodded and ended the call.

Then she walked into the kitchen and got herself a cold beer out of the fridge. She walked back into the living room, turned on the TV, and sat nursing her beer and nursing her wounds.

Tamed by Tylenol, her throbbing headache slowly subsided to something manageable.

Occasionally Isadora smiled a crazy smile to herself.

Considering what I have in mind for Joe Parker, tonight is gonna be a really long one.

CHAPTER 4

Paul & Jennifer

"I don't see why Marko can't just hire a psychic if he wants to give his creepy house a clean bill of spiritual health," Paul's girlfriend Jennifer Phipps said as they dropped the last of their things in the trunk of Paul's car, a silver BMW that had seen better days. "Spook chasers are a dime a dozen here in Boston and elsewhere."

Paul stared up at the evening sky with its layered white and gray clouds, and then he shut the car trunk. The town of Raynham, their destination, was a mere thirty-five miles south of Boston. Paul saw no need to hurry; give or take five minutes, they'd be there by dinnertime anyhow.

"I didn't bother to inquire why Marko didn't want a psychic," he told Jennifer. "And trust me, I also didn't attempt to point that obvious point out." He shrugged at her. "Would you?"

Jennifer Phipps considered his question for about a second and then shook her head. "Definitely not, if he was gonna wipe my slate clean."

Paul smiled. "My POV exactly, babe."

Not for the first time since hearing about the impromptu trip to Raynham that they'd be making, Jennifer gave Paul a confused look. "But one-fifty grand . . . that's a lot of money to forego."

Paul held Jennifer by the shoulders, his fingers tangling in her shoulder-length blonde hair, stared into her gray eyes and shrugged. "He said he's figured I'll never be able to pay him back anyway. Offering me this 'job' is Marko's way of saving face at home—he'll be able to tell my sis that he got something for his money."

Now Jennifer laughed.

Paul laughed too. "Babe, I'm just glad I'm getting this break. I'm not dumb enough to look a gift horse in the mouth. My constant fear has been that one day, Marko will get so pissed off at Petra's endless infidelities that he'll kill me instead of her to let off steam."

Paul jerked a thumb towards the front of the BMW. "Hey, let's go pick up Billy."

Once they were in the car and heading toward Billy Evans's house, Jennifer said, "You said Marko said the more the merrier. So, who else is coming along to Raynham with us?"

Paul kept his eyes on the road, and flicked the indicator for a right turn. "I dunno. Billy says he'll mention it to a college buddy or two of his and ask them to bring their girlfriends along. And I know he's got a filmmaker aunt who vlogs on occult stuff, and who may be interested in checking out the place. Whether she'll be able to make the trip on such short notice or not is of course debatable."

"This is turning into quite the party."

Paul nodded. "Well, it's on Marko's buck. We might as well enjoy ourselves. Besides, with the sort of debt relief I'm getting, we'd better give Marko value for money."

He took his eyes off the road ahead for a few moments to glance sideways at her and yell in delight: "Yoo hoo, babe, come Monday, I'll be free as the air! NO more fear that the IMF—meaning the Irate Murderous Financier—is gonna come calling."

Jennifer had heard that acronym before and rolled her eyes.

Paul returned his attention to the highway and made the coming turn. Then he asked Jennifer. "Hey, you got anyone you wanna invite out to the house? Maybe someone who lives near Raynham, and who can meet up with us without screwing up their weekend plans?"

Jennifer had just opened up TikTok on her phone. "Not really," she replied. "But I'll keep it in mind." Then her expression turned inquisitive. "Hey, don't we need to bring some cameras along? You know, to film any spooks that we find?"

Paul sighed. "No need to. There's no such things as ghosts and you can't film what doesn't exist."

"Ghosts *do* exist," Jennifer replied. "You're just too bull-headed to admit it."

Paul laughed. "Let's not go into this again. There's no such things as ghosts. All that paranormal stuff on TV that you love is all faked."

"Put your money where your mouth is," Jennifer said with a cool smile, as their car turned onto Billy Evans's street. "Let's bet on it. No ghosts in the house we're heading for and . . ."

"And what?"

"And I'll give you blowjobs twice a day for a month."

"Alright, yeah!" Paul yelped before thinking better of it.

"But if we find out that Danika Velli's new house is haunted," Jennifer added, "Then you take me on a two-week vacation to Florida. I get a six-star hotel and first-class treatment. Deal?"

"Deal," Paul agreed without hesitation. "Honey, you've already lost this one. I can already feel your sweet lips wrapped around my dick."

Jennifer, however, shook her head. "Start saving, sweetheart," she told Paul as the BMW pulled up to the side of Billy's house. "I've a weird and crazy feeling that by the end of this weekend, you'll be more of a believer in the paranormal than I am."

Billy was seated on his front porch waving at them.

Paul Dunford laughed at how easily he was certain to win his bet with Jennifer.

CHAPTER 5

Isadora & Sharday

After what felt to her like an eternity, Isadora's front doorbell buzzed.

On hearing the buzzer, Isadora leapt up from the couch, ran over to the front door and opened it up.

Then she grabbed hold of Sharday Brooks, pulled her into the house, and slammed the door shut again.

"Shit, you finally made it!" she gasped at Sharday. "What kept you?"

"Kept me?" Sharday asked in surprise, and then glanced at her wristwatch. "Dora, I said I'll be here in fifteen. I'm three minutes early."

Isadora in turn now studied the clock on the living room wall. "Yeah. I'm sorry. You're right—I'm just so damn nervous. I kept imagining Joe waking up from his drunk and coming back to kill me."

"That ain't happenin', girl," Sharday said.

Sharday Brooks was black, tall and thin, and had short-cropped hair that she'd dyed blonde. Her denim shirt and pants were masculine, and she wore calf-high workman's boots.

She had a duffel bag slung over her left shoulder.

Isadora had often joked with Sharday she looked like the stereotypical dyke. This evening though, her friend simply looked 'efficient.'

'Efficiency' was what Isadora needed right now. She intended to be supremely 'efficient' on Joe's brutal ass.

The two women walked into Isadora's living room. Isadora waited while Sharday examined her face. As Sharday's fingers traced the bruises on Isadora's cheeks and lips, her dusky face grew even darker with rage.

"Joe did this to you?" she whispered to Isadora, with additional words momentarily seeming to fail her.

Isadora nodded back. "Yes, he did, and—"

"Why is there blood on your legs? Are you on your period?"

Isadora turned around and bent over the living room couch, which itself had some splatters of blood on it. Then she spread her buttocks with her hands and said, "See for yourself, nurse."

Sharday Books *was* in fact a nurse. She worked at the Raynham Outlook Clinic.

Isadora heard Sharday's loud intake of breath.

"How bad is it back there?" Isadora asked. "It hurts to sit down."

"How *can* you even sit down?" Sharday asked sympathetically. "I should get one of my gay friends to rape Joe for doing this to you. Show *him* what it feels like to have to take this kind of treatment." Isadora felt a tap on her ass. "Okay, you can turn around now."

Isadora did. She was delighted to see the anger simmering on her friend's face. She could tell that Sharday was still enraged, but that she now had her anger under control, which, Isadora suspected, was worse for Joe.

"Okay, what do you want us to do to Joe?" Sharday whispered.

Isadora's response was to step right up to Sharday, pull her close, slip her arms around her neck, and plant her lips on Sharday's.

She felt Sharday's initial tension at the shock of the long-desired-but-never-conceded intimate contact.

However, Sharday's surprise quickly passed. Her lips softened and parted and the kiss became a mutual give and take. Sharday's arms encircled her and pulled her tight against her breasts. She felt Sharday's right knee inch up between her thighs.

They stood like that for ages, kissing and holding each other tight.

Although being held and caressed by Sharday felt wonderful, Isadora was uncertain what she was getting into. Ever since their high school days, Sharday had never made any bones about Isadora being her perfect woman, the one for whom she was prepared to move the stars from their courses if need be.

Isadora hadn't been interested; she'd wanted a man, not a woman.

And she'd been very happy with men until she'd begun dating Joe Parker.

Finally, she felt Sharday's hands on her shoulders, gently pushing her away. Isadora attempted to keep their lips in contact, but finally her tongue slipped out of Sharday's mouth, dangling a long strand of saliva in the air between them.

"Wow," the black woman said, with a confused expression on her face. "Just wow!"

"Okay, girl, I'm all yours," Isadora said, and for emphasis pinched her friend's right nipple. "We both know you want me—now you got me." Then she jerked her thumb sideways towards the hallway across the living room. "But first, you gotta help me take out the white trash."

Sharday frowned and caressed the nipple that Isadora had just pinched. "I thought you loved Joe. 'Till death do us part, remember?"

Isadora rolled her eyes. "Did I really once say that? Till death do us part? Dammit, girl, I must've meant 'till death do us fart.' Right now, I'm updating Joe and I's love life. Loving that sonofabitch any longer with surely result in my death at his hands."

"I believe you," Sharday told her, with a grim expression on her face. "Remember I'm a nurse; I gotta deal with battered women every now and then." She stepped closer and felt Isadora's face. "This is quite the black eye you got here. How'd Joe . . . ?"

"Whiskey bottle."

"Damn, he *was* trying to kill you," Sharday scowled. "You know what, honey? Let's do this."

"Yes, let's," Isadora agreed. Then she stepped up close to Sharday and kissed her again.

***

Isadora watched her new girlfriend crouch down by the duffel bag that she'd earlier dropped on the floor and begin rummaging through it.

"What exactly do you intend to do to Joe?" she asked.

Sharday's purple lips peeled back over her teeth in a smile. "Whatever *you* want, honey. He's *your* boyfriend."

"You mean ex-boyfriend."

"I forgot that for a few seconds. What sort of treatment do you want us to give him?"

"The full surgical works. He threatened to cut off my nose if I ever left him. Turn around is fair play."

Sharday stood up. Isadora saw that she was holding a hypodermic syringe. Sharday's eyes now had an intense gleam in them that Isadora had never seen in them before. The look was both exciting and scary.

"What's that stuff do?" she asked Sharday, gesturing to the syringe.

"Just a little shot to help Joe relax during his surgery." Sharday turned towards the hallway and then gestured to Isadora over her shoulder. "Come on, hon. We need to move your ex into the bathroom."

Isadora followed her with growing excitement.

Inside the bedroom, Joe was still out cold. The difference from the last time Isadora had been in here was that now he was lying on his back and his fly was open, as if he'd gotten up in the interim to use the toilet but couldn't be bothered to zip up again.

Isadora waited by the door while Sharday stepped up to the bed. Now that they were close to cutting Joe out her life, she couldn't shake the worry that something would go wrong.

Selfish reasoning or not, I'm remaining well out of reach of Joe's hands. If he grabs Sharday I'll rush over and save her.

"He didn't even bother to wash your blood and shit off his cock," Sharday told Isadora in disgust. "Men like him make me want to kill all men."

Then she turned to give Isadora a puzzled look. "His face is busted up. What happened to his nose?"

"I did."

Sharday smiled. "Good girl. You didn't just lie down and take it."

"Please hurry up and jab him before he wakes up. Remember he's bigger than both of us combined."

Joe stirred a little then, as if he'd heard what she'd said, or maybe his subconscious sensed danger nearby.

Isadora wondered why Sharday was taking so long to inject Joe with the sedative.

She seems to relish Joe's helplessness. That's a side of her I'm unfamiliar with.

Suddenly, Joe growled in his sleep like a bear who figured he'd hibernated enough. Isadora's worries returned. Joe twisted on the bed, and looked as if he might indeed wake up from sleep and attack both of them.

Isadora was just about to run back to the living room to look for Joe's switchblade, when Sharday finally jabbed Joe in the forearm with the hypo.

After she injected the pale fluid into Joe's arm, his chest seemed to inflate like a balloon, but then he subsided again and his breathing normalized.

"All done," Sharday said, after watching the prone man for a few seconds more. "Now we need to get him undressed. Where are your scissors?"

"Over there on the—"

While replying, Isadora had begun walking towards her vanity to retrieve the needed scissors, but both her reply and her walk were interrupted when Sharday grabbed her elbow and spun her around to face her.

"Hey, hey, wait up a moment," Sharday said.

Isadora waited to hear what Sharday would say.

"Are you sure that you want to go through with this?" Sharday asked, with a concerned look on her face. "I'm asking 'cos once we get started on shithead there . . ." here she paused and gestured at Joe ". . . it ain't like our lives can ever go back to normal." she peered intently into Isadora's eyes and Isadora felt her brown gaze as pressure on her brain.

"I need you to think this through properly," Sharday said. "I'm totally with you, no matter what decision you take. I just want you to be sure, before we hurt Joe, that this is really what you want to do. At the moment he's simply incapacitated. He won't remember anything if we leave him alone.

"In fact, with the way Joe is now, we can simply load all of his belongings into your car, dump him into the car along with them, and then drive him over to the Sunflower Motel. We'll rent a room there for a couple nights, dump Joe onto the bed in the room, and leave him a note informing him that you and he are now past history and also warning him that if he ever comes back . . . if he ever turns up on your doorstep again, you'll sic the cops on him."

Isadora flung an angry look at the drugged man lying in her bed. What Sharday was suggesting was so simple, so sensible, so logical, and yet so impossible.

"Shit, I really do wish I could simply walk away from this," she replied angrily. "But If I leave Joe alone, he won't leave me alone. Joe will keep on stalking me, he'll keep coming after me, until in the end, either he'll kill me or I'll kill him."

"Which means the end equals the beginning," Sharday agreed. "And the means justify the end. Okay, get the scissors. Let's get Joe naked and into the bathtub."

Feeling like a bird who's just noticed that its owner accidentally left the door of its cage open, Isadora hurried over to her dresser to get her scissors.

She didn't immediately find them. When she finally did locate the scissors in one of the dresser drawers and turned around again, she was surprised to see that during the interlude when she'd not been watching her, Sharday had stripped down to her panties.

"Don't wanna get my clothes stained with Joe's blood," Sharday explained as she began sliding her light blue panties down her dark thighs.

Isadora took a few seconds to note how fantastically tight and toned Sharday's body was, with a criminally firm belly and sweet conical breasts, before nodding that she understood.

Sharday stepped out of her panties and placed them in a pile with her other discarded clothes, then she stretched and smiled at Isadora.

"Okay, darling," she said, "let's get Joe Blow here naked and into your bathtub." She once more had that excited look in her eyes that Isadora had noticed earlier.

Sharday smiled cruelly. "And then I'll fetch my bag of surgical equipment."

CHAPTER 6

Paul, Jennifer, & Billy

Dusk had deepened when Paul Dunford drove the BMW up the long driveway of the house on Carver Street. The house was exactly like the photos Marko had sent him via WhatsApp: two stories of old-style architecture, average-sized, and surrounded by a good number of trees.

The trio's trip down south had been speedy and uneventful.

Paul had been in Raynham lots of times before. The most recent of these trips had been to attend the funeral of a friend.

That last time, Raynham had struck Paul as the sort of sleepy little town where nothing was supposed to happen, but everything did. Yes, Raynham was that kind of a place. He'd never taken the time to really work out the actual stats, but Paul knew that several times a year Raynham, MA got in the news, and what got reported was generally something supposedly inexplicable and creepy.

***

For instance, Larry Banks, the friend whose funeral Paul had been in town to attend, had died at the hands of a new urban legend called '#Bombella the Errorist.'

As the name suggested, Bombella's name was Ella and she bombed people. The difference between Bombella and regular bombers, however, was that she didn't plant bombs in public places, but instead abducted her victims and subjected them to 'personalized bombings.'

Larry Banks' case was a classic example of Bombella's modus operandi. Larry had been out having lunch with his wife and kids when he'd got up to use the restroom . . . and never returned.

No one saw him leave the restaurant, so how had he been spirited away?

Then, that night, Rita Banks had received an email titled 'Your Husband Larry's Messy End.' The email had contained a link to a webpage where a video had been uploaded.

In the video, Larry Banks had his mouth duct-taped shut and was strapped down to a chair. Rita had immediately thought there was something weird about the chair, but she'd not understood *what* until the fatal afterwards.

Bombella's digitally distorted voice now spoke. "Hello, Rita Banks," it said. "I am Bombella. I find your husband guilty of crimes against Wokeness. It's about time that he permanently woke up."

That was all Bombella said and then a woman's hand had appeared in the picture holding a black remote control unit with a red button on it.

The thumb pressed the button, and the chair that Larry was sitting on instantly exploded.

Larry, of course, blew up along with the chair. In the video, all that was left of him afterwards was a mess of minced flesh splattered all over the place.

Rita Banks had instantly called the cops. She'd managed to soldier on through the detectives' questions, but her mind had broken the next morning when after hearing a knock on their front door, her eldest son had found a white cardboard box with '#Crimes Against Wokeness' written on it in green Sharpie.

The box had contained enough of Larry Banks' remains for the police to positively confirm that Larry was in fact dead and was not merely playing a gag on his family.

Rita Banks had collapsed then and was still under intense medical supervision and psychiatric therapy.

Larry Banks was just one of numerous victims. Bombella's explosive movies depicting her other murders were available on the internet, if you knew where to look.

As to who Bombella was, or where she was, the police had no idea. All of their investigations had led to dead ends, as if the bombing victims had been murdered by someone who didn't actually exist.

Rumors now had it that Bombella was a devil who'd somehow slipped through a crack in the wall that separated Earth from hell.

Until the police could find her, however, the mystery still remained, and proved to be one more instance of the town of Raynham's morbid oddity.

***

But this house looks alright, Paul thought after he'd parked the car and they'd all gotten out of it. *Nothing creepy about this place at all. I wonder what scared Marko's mama so much.*

"This place looks creepy," Jennifer said. "No wonder old Danika Velli took a hard pass on it."

Paul smiled at his girlfriend. "Babe, I was just thinking the exact opposite."

She shook her head at him. "You've so insensitive you could be a chopping board."

Paul nodded. "Yup. And that's why the boss gave me this housesitting job."

Jennifer looked at Billy. "What's your first impression of this place? Creepy or not creepy?"

Billy shrugged. He was a regular everyday-looking kind of guy, though quite buff because he worked out. Billy was in his early twenties, fresh out of college and currently applying for jobs with the Massachusetts government. His friendship with Paul and Jennifer went back to when he used to mow their lawn for high-school pocket money.

"It's a little bit creepy," Billy replied. "But I think that's 'cos of the 1930s-style architecture. That, and all of these trees around it." He frowned. "Somehow, the trees seem out of place here; if that makes any sense to you."

Jennifer turned back to Paul with a smile. "You've been defeated two to one."

"Okay, you win." In the meantime, Paul had been staring at the two-story building and scratching his head.

Sure, this place looks ordinary, but Jen and Billy are right: there is something 'off' about it.

He gazed up at the building's dark upper-floor windows and felt an inexplicable unease. *The old architecture is one discrepant factor, and the trees are another, but there's something impossible to finger . . . nah, I'm letting Marko and Jen's superstitions freak me out. I'm better than that.*

Still, with a lingering feeling of unease, he gestured back at the BMW's trunk. "Time to unload our stuff."

Paul leaned back into the car and popped the trunk open. And then, just as he was about walking to the rear of the car with the others, his phone rang.

"It's Marko," he told them before answering.

"Evening, boss."

Marko Velli's voice came over the phone. "Hey, Paulie, just checking that you've arrived at the house."

"We have. We're getting our stuff out of the car now."

"Good, good." Marko's voice was slightly slurred as if he'd been drinking for a while. "So, everything's fine over there. Hey, what's your first impression of the place? You think it's haunted or not?"

Before replying, Paul glanced over at Jennifer and Billy. But both were preoccupied with their tasks.

"Looks normal to me so far," Paul said, lowering his voice so the others wouldn't hear him. "It's just an old house, that's all."

Marko was silent for a while, then said: "Oh yeah, there's something I forgot to tell ya. Listen, Paulie, there's something in the house that may change your mind 'bout that."

Paul was intrigued. "What?"

Marko laughed. "Alright, get this: upstairs, there's some kinda magical symbol carved into the second-floor balcony. It's really large. Huge, extends all over the balcony floor."

"Balcony? I'm looking at the house and I can't see any balcony on the second floor."

"It's at the back of the house; looks out over the backyard."

Paul digested this. "So, you're saying your house used to belong to Satanists?"

There was a pause after this. As the silence extended, Paul could almost see Marko at the other end of the line, with his brow deeply furrowed as he tried to remember the details without reaching for his cellphone.

"Aw, I think so. I don't really remember too much. The info was included with the house specs, but I didn't pay too much attention to the details. But I think that either the guy who built the place was a devil-worshipper, or his daughter was."

"That's interesting, but it doesn't mean the place is haunted," Paul said.

Marko laughed. "I admire your skepticism. I wish I didn't believe in the supernatural either. At the moment it's costing me a lot of money."

Paul looked over at Jennifer. She had a bag of groceries in her hands and once Paul caught her eye, gave him a look that asked: 'What the heck are you guys talking about? Hurry up and come help us unload.' He shrugged back at her.

"Anyway, have fun over there," Marko said. "If you meet any ghosts, take selfies with 'em and I'll upload them to my Facebook feed."

Paul chortled at the joke. "We'll try to."

"Oh, and how's it coming along with assembling more house-sitters? Like I already told ya, bring as many folks as you like—fill the house with people if you can. Don't worry 'bout them making a mess of the place—my guys will handle cleanup after they leave. What's important is that there's enough witnesses that the place is either clean or unclean, if you understand me."

"We're working on it. I'm expecting four or five more friends to arrive either tonight or tomorrow morning."

"Great, great," Marko said. "And before I hang up, there's just one more thing I gotta tell you. Listen, Paulie, I don't wanna sound like I'm flogging a dead horse here . . . but be careful over there. I mean it. Be *careful* in that house. Petra will never forgive me if I get you killed." Marko took a few audible breaths before going on: "You see, what's been eating me since I sent you off to Raynham is that . . . Well, okay, back on that day when I brought mama over to see the house, it would've made sense to me if mama had gone into the house and maybe climbed the stairs to the second floor, and then freaked out on seeing the magic symbol carved on the balcony—it's a pentagram— but she lost it before even stepping foot inside there. And you shoulda seen the old girl's face when she freaked out; it went totally bloodless. Paul, mama wasn't just being stubborn, she looked terrified."

"It was that bad?" After asking this, Paul shrugged again at Jennifer as she and Billy returned from yet another trip to drop off stuff on the front porch.

"I ain't making this stuff up," Marko replied. "She looked like she was seeing something that none of the rest of us could. So, like I said earlier, take care in there. You may not be superstitious like me, but to my reasoning, the devil don't need you to believe in his existence to be real. You get my point."

"Loud and clear," Paul agreed, while amused that Marko, who was possibly the most brutal man that Paul had met in his life, was giving him this advice.

"Okay, you can go now," Marko said. "Get back to me if you need more money or anything, and I'll send it over."

And on that note, Marko Velli hung up the phone.

Paul put his phone away, and stared at the house with fresh respect. *You used to belong to devil worshippers?*

Then he turned around and went to give Jennifer and Billy a hand with unloading the car.

"Any updates from your friend Aaron?" Paul asked Billy while they carried stuff over to the front porch.

"Yep, Aaron's confirmed they'll be here in about two hours. They're driving in from Springfield. He's still waiting for his friends to get to his place."

"How many people are there in his party? So, we can prepare for them?"

"Four, I think. He, Tom, and two chicks."

Paul nodded. He felt pleased. Marko would be delighted to have this many naysayers to pooh-pooh his mother's reservations.

But then Paul noticed Jennifer smiling at him, one of those sorts of smiles that assured him something had gone wrong.

"What's the matter, babe?" he asked her. "We didn't forget the house keys, did we?" While asking this, Paul instinctively patted down his leather jacket to confirm that the keys were in his pockets. He felt a moment's panic on discovering they weren't there, but then remembered he'd put them in the glove compartment.

So, what's Jenny concerned about?

"We forgot the beer," Jennifer told him.

Oh that.

Paul shrugged. "Let's just get the stuff into the house first. There's that liquor store over on Broadway that we can buy drinks from. No need to take the car even; we'll just walk over there."

CHAPTER 7

Sharday & Isadora

"Damn he's heavy!" Sharday gasped after she and Isadora had successfully manhandled Joe into the bathtub. When they let go of Joe, his head cracked back loudly against the rim of the tub.

Isadora winced at the loudness of the noise. Joe's face was already messy with the blood from his broken nose, and Isadora suspected that they might just have popped the rear of his head open also.

Sharday however, laughed. "Sorry, Joe," she said. "But right now, you getting a concussion is the least of your worries."

Sharday left the room to fetch her duffel bag. Once she returned with it, both women sat on the edge of the bathtub to catch their breath.

This is so surreal, Isadora thought. *Three of us naked in the bathroom like we're gonna fuck. But oh no, that definitely ain't happening tonight.*

Sex or no sex, she smiled at the thought, and studied Sharday's body. She felt a moment's thrill on remembering that Sharday's body was now hers.

Not like I ever wanted it before tonight. But, now it's like her body is mine whether I want it or not, so I'd better enjoy it.

Isadora shifted her attention to Sharday's face. Sharday was staring down at Joe with merciless eyes. Joe too, was staring back up at her. The expression in his eyes was unreadable. His lips moved like he was trying to speak, however.

Whatever Sharday had shot him up with had stolen control of his limbs from him.

The fact that Joe was still awake bothered Isadora.

"Hey, isn't he supposed to be unconscious?" she asked.

"Not from the small dose I gave him. He's already drunk, so I only injected sufficient of the sedative to temporarily paralyze his muscles. This way, he'll feel everything we do to him." She stared earnestly at Isadora. "You do want him to hurt, don't you?"

Isadora nodded. "Oh yes, yes. I want him to hurt like he's hurt me, and I want him to feel every damn thing that we do to him."

33

She emphasized the 'every damn thing,' while leaning over Joe and staring deep into his eyes, just like she used to do while having an orgasm, back when they were still madly in love.

When she straightened up again, she saw that Sharday was holding up a portable blowtorch that she'd clearly pulled out of her carryall.

"Let's get started then, shall we?" Sharday said, firing up the blowtorch.

"What are you gonna do . . .?"

But before she finished asking the question, Sharday leaned forward and set Joe's hair on fire with the blowtorch flame.

She did so carefully, sweeping the blowtorch over Joe's head just enough so that his hair caught fire and then quickly moving the flame away. And then, while his hair lit up like a candle flame, she moved the blowtorch lower and set his mustache and beard on fire also.

Burning his mustache fried the flesh between his nose and upper lip.

Because of the blood that had gotten in it from his broken nose, his beard took slightly longer to light up, but finally it gave in to the flame also.

Suddenly, Joe's head seemed surrounded by a halo.

Sharday killed the blowtorch flame. "Behold the patron saint of wife-beaters," she declaimed in a mocking voice.

Joe of course couldn't move; the best he could do was squirm as the fire burnt around his face. His eyes rolled crazily in their sockets and his feet kicked weakly.

Isadora wrinkled her nose. The burning hair smelt horrible. She was relieved when the fire burnt out.

She liked the result though. Once they brushed the hair-ash away, the entirety of Joe's scalp and chin (and the front part of his neck also) looked roasted; the skin was either peeled off or cracked and seeping fluid.

"What do you think?" Sharday asked Isadora seriously. "Am I a good hairdresser, or what?"

Isadora stepped close to her and hugged her. "The best! Just look at his face."

"I think he wants to apologize to you. Hey, Joe, do you wanna apologize to Isadora?"

Joe looked at the ceiling and looked like shit.

"Alright, so that's the first thing done," Sharday told Isadora.

"What's next?" Isadora asked.

"One moment please." Sharday put down the blowtorch next to her bag and rummaged through it again. This time, when she straightened up, she was holding a leather folder that contained scalpels. "When, I arrived here tonight, your ass was bleeding," Sharday said, slipping one of the scalpels out from the folder and twisting it in the light. "So, I think a little bit of payback is due to Joe."

Isadora shivered. "We're gonna cut his dick off?"

Sharday grinned at her. "Hell no, hon. We're just gonna make him wish we would cut his dick off."

The answer confused Isadora. "How the hell are we gonna accomplish that?"

"Wait and see." Then Sharday gestured at her. "Grab the head of his dick and pull it out straight."

When Isadora took hold of Joe's penis, she felt the return of her anger at him. The penis was still covered with her blood. That fact alone brought home to her how much Joe deserved what they were going to do to him now.

"Pull it out a bit more," Sharday told her, "and make sure not to let go once I start cutting on it."

"Ugh!" Isadora said. Joe's dick was of course as limp as it could possibly be. She looked up at Joe, whose lips were trembling furiously now, and between whose lips the pink tongue slipped in and out like a confused snake.

Yeah, he's really trying to tell us something. He really is.

Sharday placed the scalpel at the base of Joe's penis and began cutting.

Isadora nudged Sharday with her elbow. "Hey. You said we aren't going to castrate him."

"We aren't. Just watch and learn."

Isadora watched while Sharday traced the scalpel blade in a circle around the base of Joe's penis, making a very shallow incision that only pierced the skin. Isadora noted that Sharday was especially careful not to nick the fat vein atop the penis, instead cutting upward into Joe's pubic hair to avoid making accidental contact with the blood vessel.

Blood from the circular wound dribbled over Sharday's hands.

Isadora cringed at the sight, but nonetheless held on to the glans of Joe's penis and tugged firmly on it to keep the organ straightened out.

There was a lot of blood. But not as much blood as there was when Sharday began peeling back Joe's penis skin like it was a condom. Now the blood squirted upward onto her breasts.

Fuck, this is nasty to watch!

But she watched on. In a horrible way, this horrible payback was fun. If she had any doubts about her enjoyment, they left her the moment she looked at Joe's eyes. Joe's eyes showed her that he was in hell. That was priceless to Isadora.

Sharday took her time with peeling away Joe's penile covering. Her delaying was clearly intended to prolong their victim's torment. Isadora wondered if the extended duration of this particular torture was for her own benefit or for Sharday's.

I hate Joe and she's a dyke. Same difference.

Occasionally, Sharday assisted the skin's removal with the scalpel, cutting through stubborn resistance.

Finally, she got it all the way up to the glans. Joe's cock now looked like an unfried sausage. It dripped blood down Isadora's fingers and onto Joe's crotch and the floor of the bathtub.

Isadora, still keeping the penis outstretched with a thumb and forefinger clamped around its head, now asked: "So what now? Oh, this is so deliciously fucked up."

Sharday chuckled. "Now, I give Joe a reverse circumcision."

"What the hell is that?"

"Honey, just watch me. Keep on holding that dick out straight like that."

Isadora had imagined that Sharday would continue peeling off the penis-skin, but instead, she now cut around and behind the glans and then, after putting down her scalpel and taking over control of the glans from Isadora, she peeled the tube of skin forward over the head of Joe's penis and slipped it completely off of the organ.

"Ha ha ha ha ha!" Isadora said, rocking back with laughter and pointing at Joe.

Either her mockery or Joe's agony triggered something in him and at that very moment, Joe's bladder gave way and he pissed himself, a long thick amber stream that, because Sharday was still holding onto his dick (and examining it as if she couldn't understand why penises had such evil power over women) resulted in the jet of piss going straight into Isadora's mouth and up her nose.

Isadora was enraged by this.

"Gimme that!" she sputtered in anger with urine pouring from her mouth. Then she snatched the wet mass of removed penis skin from Sharday's grasp.

Isadora next violently shoved the penis skin into Joe's mouth. "Eat this, cocksucker!"

Joe, of course, couldn't bite her, and she intended to shove his dick-skin down his throat, but suddenly, she felt Sharday's hands pulling her away from Joe.

"Hey, what . . .?" she protested angrily as Sharday turned her around, but the next moment Sharday pulled her in close and locked her lips with hers, and Isadora's rage faded away and was replaced by desire, particularly once Sharday's fingers began playing between her legs. Faster and faster and faster, until Isadora felt herself dissolving, melting away into a nerveless pool of peace and contentment.

Once her orgasm was over, she fell limp against Sharday, who now carefully eased both of their bodies down till they were both sitting on the rim of the bathtub again.

"I had piss in my mouth when you kissed me," Isadora said. "You didn't care about that?"

"I'd have kissed you if you had shit in your mouth," Sharday replied. "I love you."

At first Isadora smiled with delighted understanding of the sincerity and depth of her new lover's feelings for her. But then, she frowned and gestured down at Joe. "Why did you stop me just now? Don't tell me you're feeling sorry for him?"

Sharday shook her head. "Oh, no. But if you choke him to death on his dick skin, we won't be able to have any more fun with him, will we?"

Isadora realized that Sharday was right. She glanced dismissively at Joe, whose skinned manhood now looked like German bratwurst, and burst out laughing.

CHAPTER 8

Isadora & Sharday

Isadora felt ecstatic about the agony that they'd so far inflicted on Joe.

Somewhere in her mind, she understood that they'd gone too far, that normal people—folks with any kind of sense of empathy for others—didn't do horrible stuff like this to people.

But she shrugged that thin whip of conscience away.

And normal men don't beat up women till they're half-dead either.

While Sharday fished about in her bag of torturous wonders for her next magic trick, Isadora studied Joe's crotch. She was impressed by how expertly Sharday had skinned Joe's penis. Though Joe's cock now resembled a skinned rabbit hanging in a butcher shop, the bleeding was minimal, just a shallow crimson pool under his ass and some splatter on the bathtub's cream-colored sides.

She looked from Joe's dick to his head, and giggled. Joe's scalp was the color of a well-done steak. And best of all, the penis skin that she'd shoved between his lips was still there, dangling bloodily from the right corner of his mouth.

"What do you intend to do with that?" Isadora asked Sharday, when she saw the large clawhammer the black woman was now holding.

Sharday stared at their victim for a while before replying. Both women were still sitting on the edge of the bathtub and Isadora stared down at Sharday's dusky thighs with a faint renewal of desire.

I wonder if she feels sexually frustrated. Sharday has a sort of nervous tension about her that suggests she needs to orgasm. I've never eaten pussy before, but it doesn't seem that hard to do. So, later then.

Isadora slid her fingers over the metal head of the hammer in Sharday's hands like it was Sharday's clitoris.

"What are you—I mean, we, of course—what're we gonna do with that?" she asked again.

"We need this to destroy the evidence," was Sharday's reply.

Isadora couldn't find an appropriate response to this, and waited while Sharday explained: "Aside from facial recognition and DNA evidence, there's two other major ways that the cops can identify a corpse. The first one is—"

Isadora interrupted her with a giggle.

"What's funny?"

"You just said: '*Cops* identify a *corpse*.' I like that play on words. Makes it sound like the police and the stiff are related in some way."

"Oh, okay. One way is through dental records and the other is through fingerprints." She stroked the hammer and then pointed it at Joe's head. "We'll deal with his fingers later. This baby is for preventing dental analysis."

On hearing this, Joe's eyes widened in their sockets. Isadora was surprised by how emotional and worried her ex suddenly seemed. She understood that Joe must be putting in a lot of effort to overcome the shot he'd been given.

"But . . . if we're going to pull his teeth, wouldn't pliers be better for the job? Joe has tools in the garage."

Sharday shook her head. "Pulling out his teeth one at a time will take too long." She weighed the hammer in her hand and explained some more: "What *you're* gonna do is *knock* his teeth out of his mouth with the hammer."

"Huh? Me?"

Sharday held the hammer out to her. "Do it. For *us*. For our new beginning. For our *love*."

Sharday had such an intense and passionate look on her face while saying this, that Isadora began wondering if maybe she wasn't exactly right in the head.

Maybe I'd have been better off simply running away from Joe and taking my chances with law enforcement.

But she knew it was already too late for that. Even if they could undo everything else, they couldn't undo the fact that they'd premeditatedly mutilated Joe.

She doubted there was any easy surgical fix for his skinned dick.

No matter how much abuse I claim in court, there's no way under heaven that Sharday at least won't be going to jail for a LONG time for what we've already done tonight.

And so, I can't back out now. If I do, the intense love she's just professed for me will very likely metamorphose into just-as-intense hatred and I'll wind up looking worse than Joe does. She's not gonna let me turn her into the police, that's for sure.

She accepted the hammer from Sharday's hand.

To be fair to Sharday, this is as much my fault as hers, even more so. Firstly, I'm the one who called her up and asked her to help me dispose of Joe. And secondly, right before we did this, she did ask me if I was certain I wanted to go through with it. Sharday gave me every chance to back out then, but I didn't. So, I'm not about to chicken out on her now.

"Listen, you're the one with medical slash dental expertise," she told Sharday. "How do I knock his teeth out with this thing?"

Sharday smiled. "Swing at his mouth from the sides. Hit him hard; the way he used to hit you, when he had the power over you."

Isadora smirked down at Joe. "Hit him the way he used to hit me? Oh, this is gonna be too damn easy then."

Sharday got up and out of Isadora's way.

Isadora grinned down at Joe. "Okay, baby, I think you've already figured out that there's no way you're gonna survive tonight."

She swung the hammer down at him. With a crack like shattering glass, the hammer hit him between the lips.

Isadora examined the damage. She'd created a hole in the middle of Joe's mouth; an empty hole devoid of all his incisors. However, there wasn't much blood, and this disappointed her until she figured that the reason why this was so, was because Joe was most likely swallowing the blood, which was naturally flowing backwards into his throat.

Satisfied by this damage that she'd inflicted on Joe, Isadora swung the hammer again. The original hole widened, and this time, when she jerked the hammer back out of his face, it came along with several white chunks of tooth.

She realized that this time she'd hit him with the claw end of the hammer. The hammer had also ripped his lips in two, granting her a clear view into the hell she'd made of his jaws, and starting crimson freshets dribbling down his chin.

"You're doing great," Sharday said encouragingly. "Hold on, let me collect his teeth."

Isadora waited while Sharday fished about in Joe's mouth for the fragments of tooth, which she secured in a small transparent plastic bag.

"There's one or two missing," she said as she worked. "I think he's swallowed them."

"Can't those be used as evidence against us?"

"Don't worry about it. After he's dead, we'll fish them out of his throat."

When Sharday was done with picking up the dislodged teeth, she nodded at Isadora. "You can go on."

But Isadora shook her head at Sharday. "Not yet. Help me sit him up in the bathtub. I can't get at his side teeth from this angle."

After she'd basked in Sharday's look of admiration, they both womanhandled Joe up to a sitting position.

"Now it's molar time!" Isadora announced excitedly and swung the hammer at Joe's head.

She'd swung the hammer without bothering to alter her grip on it, meaning that this time too, she hit Joe's face with its claw side. She also miscalculated and instead of knocking his molars into his mouth, wound up digging into his left ear. Isadora ripped the hammer back and ended up clawing off Joe's entire left ear and a fair amount of his cooked scalp.

Blood spurted from the wound and splattered Isadora's belly.

Sharday stared with bemusement at the ear on the end of the hammer.

Isadora giggled. "You know what they say: Practice makes perfect."

"Practice away, baby," Sharday said. "I gotta take a shit."

While Sharday sat on the toilet and grunted like she'd had chili con carne for breakfast, lunch, and dinner for the past fortnight, Isadora got to work with ridding her ex of the rest of his teeth.

Once she'd knocked all of his left-side premolars and molars into the middle of his mouth, she took a break and studied Sharday on the toilet. She'd never watched another woman poop before and doing so felt like she was watching herself. The smell was the same anyway.

"You look miserable," she told Sharday.

"Not as miserable as we're gonna be if you don't finish getting out his teeth. I know we're both lesbians now; but we don't wanna be *prison* lesbians."

Isadora turned around and frowned down at Joe's ruined face. He didn't have much of a mouth anymore—just a mess of pulped and torn-up flesh and shattered bone that would give any dentist nightmares for life.

And the blood! There's do damn much of it.

Isadora recalled once having a molar pulled, and the dentist's warning to her to visit the ER if the bleeding didn't subside after a reasonable period of time, or if it resumed after it had stopped.

And Joe's mouth is bleeding enough for all the patients in Dr. Fowler's waiting room.

She gaped into Joe's mouth (which was easy to do because the hammer had torn his left cheek to shreds) and studied the white objects that were piled up on his tongue. The teeth were all bloody and most of them still had some flesh attached. Several of them were incomplete, with the other half sticking out of his gums, gums that were themselves warped into morbid shapelessness. One or two of Joe's teeth had stuck in his throat again.

Isadora fished in Joe's mouth for the teeth and put them away in the plastic bag. One of the teeth that she pulled out came along with a long strip of flesh that was still anchored inside Joe's mouth. Isadora was initially going to search inside Sharday's bag for a knife to cut through the strip, but she suddenly changed her mind and instead threaded the dangling tooth out through Joe's savaged cheek and let it dangle down on his neck.

"Hey, get back to work!" Sharday grunted.

"Don't bitch at me 'cos your ass is on fire," Isadora retorted. "It's not my fault you love spicy food so much."

Still, she got back to work.

Knocking out the rest of Joe's teeth was more difficult, as the right side of his head faced the wall and as such was out of the direct range of her hammer swings, but Isadora found a workaround.

She got up to her feet and bent Joe's head over so that it was lying on the outer rim of the bathtub.

Touching him enabled her to understand exactly how much damage she was doing to him. His body trembled like Jell-O, and he was sweating bullets.

And the shit smell in the bathroom had doubled; Isadora didn't know if that was entirely Sharday's fault, or if pain had caused Joe's ass to loosen up and had made him empty his bowels.

Now that Joe's head was properly positioned for her, Isadora bludgeoned his jaw from above.

SMACK! SMACK! More SMACK!

As she worked, blood squirted up into her face, but she persevered with her task.

After a few more horrendous cracks coming from Joe's jaw, she was done. She peeked through the fresh hole in Joe's right cheek and was surprised to discover that she could see the wall of the bathtub through the other side of his face. Some of the teeth that she'd just knocked out were perched on Joe's tongue, while some had fallen out of his mouth altogether through that lower hole.

As to the condition of Joe's jaw, Isadora was struck by the thought that she'd done so much damage to it that she might be able to pull it off of Joe's face entirely if she wanted to. She decided not to make an attempt at doing so.

She considered her own body. Her breasts and shoulders were drenched in blood. A glance in the medicine cabinet mirror confirmed that her face was almost as bloody as her body.

"He's bleeding a lot," she worriedly told Sharday, who was now wiping her ass clean.

Sharday dropped the used toilet paper into the toilet bowl and then flushed. "Fuck him. It don't matter if he bleeds to death. We're gonna kill him anyway."

Isadora dropped the hammer on top of Joe and now held the plastic bag containing his teeth up to the light and tried to count them.

"Seems like they're all here," she said. "He was missing two teeth and I think he swallowed three of them."

She turned around to see Sharday spraying the bathroom with air freshener. Glad to be rid of the atrocious fecal smell, she inhaled the jasmine-and-orange fragrance deeply.

"Okay, now let's get rid of Joe's fingerprints," Sharday told her.

Isadora leaned over and kissed Sharday. "I utterly adore how twisted you are," she told her afterwards.

CHAPTER 9

Paul, Jennifer, & Billy

While Billy moved their luggage off of the front porch and into the house, Paul and Jennifer walked back to the car to fetch the last of their bags.

"I still can't believe we forgot to pack all our booze," Paul said laughing. "Just imagine if this had been a camping trip; it would've been one hell of a dry weekend."

"It's 'cos you aren't that much of a drinker," Jennifer told him, hooking her arm in his.

"I guess there's something to be said for being an alcoholic after all. Good thing the—huh?"

They'd just stepped around the rear of the BMW to find a woman standing there.

Paul gaped at her. Jennifer gave a small yelp of fright and instinctively stepped backward.

Okay, so with the trunk up and the sun going down there's no way we'd have noticed her till we got here, but I'd've sworn she wasn't anywhere nearby . . . like out on the sidewalk . . . a short while ago.

Paul forced away the disturbing thought of 'ghost' that immediately came to his mind and then glanced across the road, at the bungalow opposite their house.

Okay, she must be the neighbor lady.

"Hello," the woman said with a smile. "I'm Phoenix Aurora. I'm sorry if I startled you."

"That's okay," Paul said, gesturing at the house opposite. "We just didn't notice you crossing the road." He extended his hand. "I'm Paul and this is Jennifer."

She shook both of their hands.

Phoenix Aurora was tall and slim and dressed completely in clothes that were as black as her hair. Black blouse, long black skirt, black boots. Her skin was as white as the moon, her eyes as blue as noonday sky, and her lips red like sunset.

Maybe it was the effect of the fading daylight, but Paul couldn't tell how old she was. Phoenix Aurora could have been thirty or forty-five, or sixty years old.

Paul found her creepy. Beautiful *and* creepy.

Shaking her hand made him feel weird. Her hand was small with long fingers. Touching her flesh did something to him that he didn't like.

When her fingers and palm touched his, he had a temporary sense of spatial dislocation. During that brief period of contact, Paul had the impression that Phoenix Aurora was in no hurry to let go of his hand. There was nothing obvious in this, nothing that, for instance, would've given Jennifer any red flags that the other woman might be interested in her boyfriend. But Paul felt like she'd gripped his hand for an eternity, when in reality it was only for two or three seconds.

And then, the seemingly endless contact was broken and Phoenix Aurora was pumping Jennifer's hand instead.

I guess I find her disorienting 'cos she's so damn pretty.

But Paul knew it was more than the woman's good looks that bothered him.

What sort of name is Phoenix Aurora anyway?

"We're just here for the weekend," Jennifer told Phoenix Aurora, while Paul struggled to get a hold on himself. It was hard going, as if shaking the woman's hand had cast a spell over him that he was fighting to throw off.

Must be a man-and-woman thing. Jenny doesn't seem affected in the least by her own handshake.

"We appreciate you coming over to say hello," Jennifer said. "It's always nice to know that the neighbors are friendly."

Phoenix Aurora laughed. "I need to properly explain my presence here. I'm not Mrs. Shipley, your neighbor across the street. I'm your housekeeper. I come with the house."

This information jerked Paul properly back to reality.

"Housekeeper?" Jennifer asked.

The woman nodded.

"M-m-marko didn't s-s-say anything about a housekeeper," Paul sputtered.

Phoenix Aurora nodded again. "I suspect he didn't know either." She gestured randomly up at the sky. "Don't worry about it. It's an old family tradition that extends back to when the house was built in the 1920s, or at least until David De Mornay bought it, back in the thirties. Because Mr. De Mornay travelled a lot, my family was employed to look after the place in his absence. And we still do. I don't live here—my house is further down the road, but I stop by from time to time to make sure the house is doing okay. Just letting you know that I'm available to cook and clean for you if you need me to."

'Make sure the house is doing okay' struck Paul as an odd statement, as if she considered the house a person.

He glanced at the house in question. "The 1920s? This building is that old?"

Phoenix's opportunity to answer was prevented by Billy joining them by the car and his being introduced to Phoenix Aurora.

Paul studied Billy's face closely while the younger man shook the housekeeper's hand, looking to see if Billy showed a similar state of distraction to that which he'd felt when he'd touched her.

But no, other than the usual delight men show on meeting pretty women for the first time, Billy seemed normal enough.

And she didn't seem to grasp the kid's hand for too long either. But maybe she didn't grasp my hand for long too; maybe my mind is playing tricks on me. I think I need a drink.

"I heard you saying something about the house," Billy said when the introductions were over. "I heard a rumor that it's haunted; how true is that?"

"Yeah, maybe you can tell us something about that," Jennifer added.

Phoenix Aurora's lips turned down in a dismissive scowl. "Oh, I know all of the rumors and stories, but I don't believe the house is haunted or cursed or whatever other nonsense they say about it." She shrugged. "I should know, right? I've worked in there for years and nothing bad has ever happened to me. I've never seen any ghosts either."

Aware that they had no need to remain by the car and that they'd be a lot more comfortable inside the house, because now the weather was becoming cold, Paul put down the car trunk and gestured towards the building.

"I wonder how this house got its spooky reputation then," Billy said as they walked towards the building.

"It was because of that nasty porno actress," Phoenix explained with a shake of her head.

"What porno actress?" Jennifer asked. They stopped by the front porch steps and looked at her.

"Lulu Moorcock," Phoenix said. "You guys never heard of her?"

"I'm not that into porn," Jennifer said. "I leave that stuff to Paul and his friends."

Phoenix laughed. "It happened back in the late seventies. Lulu Moorcock was a fast-rising porno star, and according to police accounts, after a promising start in the adult film business—for instance, she got to work with both John Holmes and Harry Reems—after that great beginning, she began doing more drugs than she could handle and became a hot mess. Then Lulu's looks started leaving her too and the film directors would no longer hire her, and so she left New York City and came to Raynham to live with her older sister and her family, who lived in this very house.

"Unfortunately though, Lulu had also started worshipping the devil along the way. So, although she was supposedly in Raynham to rehab, in actuality, she was staying with her sister Monica Sommet because Monica had three adolescent virgin daughters."

"Shit," Paul said, his lips twisting up in a grimace. "Does the rest of this story go according to the regular horror script?"

Beside him, Jennifer had an 'ick!' look on her face too.

"Perfectly to script," Phoenix Aurora said with a nod and a cold smile on her face. "From what was later discovered, Lulu's Satanist friends had assured her that if she sacrificed three virgins, Satan would grant her her looks back and in addition make her the world's number one adult actress." Phoenix laughed. "And so, there was a slaughter. One night in August of that year, five or six people reportedly broke into this very house and butchered the entire family. All three virgin girls were reportedly raped with knives until they died from blood loss."

"I think I'm gonna be sick," Jennifer said, and grabbed hold of Paul, who looked worriedly at her in case she was serious about throwing up.

The housekeeper smiled sympathetically at Jennifer. "The story's almost over," she said. "The entire murdered family of five were arranged around the giant pentagram that's carved into the upper balcony, and Lulu was sitting in the middle of the pentagram. That's how the police found them all the next day, after Mr. Sommet, who was the headmaster of the local elementary school, didn't show up to work. The other Satanist killers were nowhere to be found."

"Fuck!" Billy said. "No wonder people think the house is cursed."

"But what happened to Lulu?" Paul asked. "You said the cops found her sitting with the bodies. Why didn't she run away?" He frowned. "Hey, don't tell me she overdosed or something."

"I hope she did," Jennifer said with feeling. "A bitch like that deserves to overdose."

Before replying, Phoenix Aurora laughed, a cold and mirthless expression that made the falling night feel incredibly cold around Paul.

"No, no, Lulu Moorcock wasn't dead," Phoenix finally told them. "She didn't flee from the scene because she'd gone insane, apparently during the magic ritual. The cops found her up on the balcony, surrounded by corpses and eating her own shit, while singing praises to the devil for making her beautiful once more."

"Great! Good riddance," Jennifer said.

"And there was one more detail," the housekeeper added with a twist of her lips.

"What?" Billy and Jennifer both asked at once.

"Apparently the ritual worked," Phoenix said. "When the police found Lulu Moorcock, despite being smeared in her own shit, she looked absolutely gorgeous and ravishing, with absolutely no signs of the ravages that her extreme heroin addiction—along with her overindulgence in other narcotics—had wrought on her body. Even her bad teeth were renewed." Phoenix giggled. "And as far as I know, Lulu Moorcock is still alive in her padded cell somewhere, still eating her own poopoo and praising Satan for making her the world's most beautiful woman. And legend has it that despite her age, her beauty refuses to fade."

"If that happened in the seventies, by now she'll be the world's oldest most beautiful woman," Billy said with a look of disgust on his face.

Paul felt just as disgusted.

What kind of woman rapes three young girls with a knife, just to restore her own looks?

"A geriatric beauty queen," Jennifer said with a disbelieving shake of her head.

"So that's how the belief that this house is cursed got started," Phoenix Aurora said. "And you know how folks are; once they're expected to see supernatural phenomena, then they'll surely do so. But like I said: I've been working here for years and I never once saw a ghost. It's a nice house, just a bit temperamental."

Hey, there she goes again, speaking about this building as if it's a person, Paul thought.

He turned to look at Jennifer, who was pulling her cellphone from her pocket. "You okay?" he asked.

"Yeah," she replied. "That is one creepy story. I wanna store Lulu's and her sister's names so I can research on it later. I might post about it on my blog."

"Huh?" Billy said like something had surprised him.

Paul looked over at Billy. "Dude, what's up?"

Billy gave him a confused look. "Where'd Phoenix go?"

His question made Paul realize that he, Billy, and Jennifer were now the only ones standing by the front porch.

Billy said, "I turned away from Phoenix to examine something down in the grass over there, and when I looked back at her, she wasn't here any longer."

"We weren't looking either," Paul told him, starting to share some of Billy's alarm. The tale about Lulu Moorcock had gotten to him.

Billy stood there scratching his head and staring out at the street, where a red car was rolling past. "But, I only looked away for a second or two. I didn't . . . I mean, that's not long enough to . . ."

"Calm down," Jennifer softly admonished the young man. "The woman can't have vanished into thin air. Peek around the side of the house, see if she's there."

Paul watched Billy walk off around the side of the house.

I know what the kid was thinking while he was looking over at the road like that. Billy was thinking that one or two seconds, or even five or ten, isn't enough time to walk down to the street and out of view along the sidewalk. So, if Phoenix isn't around the side of the house, where the hell did Phoenix go?

After about a minute, Billy walked back into view again, this time emerging around the opposite corner of the house from that which he'd begun his search.

"She's not there," he announced, needlessly, because the perplexed look on his face already told Paul that much.

Paul shrugged. "Well, there has to be some kind of a logical explanation to her sudden disappearance. Maybe she slipped away into the woods or something."

Billy looked unconvinced. "You really think so?"

Jennifer laughed. "Kid, you heard that creepy story the lady just told us. How better to put an exclamation point to it, than to pretend to go missing?"

Paul laughed too. "Relax, Billy, you felt how solid she was, didn't you? Don't lie that your wiener didn't get hard when she shook your hand."

Just like he'd hoped it would, that piece of info got through to Billy, who visibly lost his state of nervous tension that had plagued him since Phoenix Aurora's inexplicable departure.

"Yeah, I guess you're right," Billy agreed. "She wasn't a ghost. She was as solid as you and me." Smiling as if from a pleasant memory, he climbed up the front porch steps, picked up two grocery bags, and carried them into the house.

Paul watched the kid depart and then suddenly, he realized that Jennifer was staring angrily up at him.

"What?"

"And you—did *your* wiener get hard too when she shook your hand?" Jennifer asked with jealous eyes.

Paul did the only thing he could. He leaned forward and kissed Jennifer. She tried to squirm away from the contact, but he pulled her body tight against his and kept his lips pressed to hers until he felt her relax and her tongue began playing inside his mouth in return.

Damn, the kid had me rattled too for a moment there, he thought while they kissed. *But, I gotta be strong here. There's no such things as ghosts. I know that. I just need to convince the others of that fact.*

CHAPTER 10

Isadora & Sharday

Joe Parker died while Isadora and Sharday were slicing his fingertips off.

"It's the only foolproof way to prevent fingerprint ID," Sharday explained. "You make a cut right here"—she demonstrated while cutting into the skin just beneath the first knuckle of Joe's right thumb—"then you slice along both sides and around in front, below the fingernail, like this, and then you lift the entire fingerprint off."

'Lifting the fingerprint off' always involved some additional cutting to free the skin from stubborn underlying flesh, and of course, Joe's blood flowed freely during this nasty procedure, squirting and dribbling over both women's bodies till they even more messy than previously.

The floor of the bathtub was now pooled with blood an inch deep. But then, Joe was a big guy; he had lots of blood in his body.

The removed 'fingerprints' were stored in the same bag as Joe's removed teeth.

To get the job properly done, both women were kneeling in the bathtub. Isadora was positioned directly on top of Joe, while Sharday was kneeling by his legs. Isadora's left foot was stuck in Joe's ruined mouth. Occasionally she intentionally kicked him in the mouth. Several times she felt her big toe hit him deep in the throat, felt its toenail ripping his flesh and starting an additional spill of blood in there.

I just want him to suffer, she thought while she and Sharday trimmed the last vestiges of identity from him.

Then all of a sudden, just as they'd finished skinning Joe's right pinky and were preparing to start on doing the same to his left thumb, Joe began violently twitching.

"Looks like the shot is finally wearing off," Isadora said.

But Sharday shook his head. "Nah, he's about dying."

This information excited Isadora no end. Shoving her girlfriend out of the way, she jerked her toes out of Joe's mouth, leapt up, and turned herself around.

"What's the matter with you?" Sharday asked, after almost cracking her head on the wall.

"I want to look into his eyes while he dies," Isadora explained. "He owes me that much."

"Well, you're right on time for a front row show," Sharday said. "From the way his body is jerking about now—I'd say he's got maybe two minutes of life left in him."

Isadora knelt down on Joe again, this time with her toes in his crotch. She settled down comfortably and watched. Joe was still jerking, but he subsided a little when he saw she was looking at him.

Maybe he thinks I feel sorry for what I've done to him. In your dreams, Joe!

By this point, Joe looked more like a movie monster than a person. His eyes were glassy, and yet still bore the barest flicker of life.

Isadora once more considered that Joe's lower jaw seemed so loose that she might as well tug it free of his face.

Her fingers twitched in anticipation of this additional violence. It felt like her hands had a mind of their own and wanted to have a go at ripping Joe's jaw off.

But if I concentrate on doing that, I may miss the great moment when he dies.

So, Isadora watched and waited.

And then it happened. As surely as sunrise and sunset, Isadora caught it—that exact moment when Joe's lifeforce left him; that moment when, like flicking off a light bulb, Joe's eyes went from 'glassy' to 'dead.'

Suddenly his eyes were no longer the windows to his soul because his soul had fled.

Now his eyes were simply wet balls in his face.

Wow! Isadora thought. She had no idea what to feel. She however felt—no, she *knew* that by experiencing this she'd been altered in some unalterable way, that she was no longer the same woman she'd been earlier today, and that she would never be that woman again.

"Wow!" she said. "That was just fantastic."

"What exactly killed him?" she asked. "Was it the blood loss from his dick, or his jaw, or his hands, even?"

"Does it matter? What matters is that he'll never ever rape your ass again with his dick, or call you a useless whore with that mouth, or beat you up again with those hands."

Laughing, they finished stripping the corpse of fingerprint evidence and then both climbed out of the bathtub.

Sharday stood staring at the corpse for a few seconds, with her brow wrinkled up in thought, then she leaned over Joe's head and began slicing what remained of his face off of his head.

"Just to ensure that he can't ever be identified," she told Isadora over her shoulder.

When Sharday held up the flesh mask that she'd trimmed off of Joe's skull, Isadora concluded that her girlfriend was nuts.

But she's a comforting and satisfying sort of nuts, like walnuts or almonds.

Sharday was holding the mask between them, and purely as an instinctive response, Isadora found herself looking through the mask's jagged eye holes at Sharday's face. As Isadora stared through those holes at Sharday's eyes, she felt like she was looking at her own death.

Like my past died tonight. No, that's not how I feel. Actually, I feel like I'm already dead for doing all of this to Joe, but just don't realize it yet.

Sharday took her time with slicing the removed face into strips and then little pieces, before securing those pieces in the same bag that held Joe's teeth and 'fingerprints.'

"Now we're good," Sharday said with a cold smile.

"What now?" Isadora asked. "We bag him up and throw him away?" The question sounded dumb to her. She knew that one didn't just throw a mutilated human corpse away, into a dumpster for instance, and expect the world to applaud.

Sharday had begun rummaging in her capacious bag again. She paused and looked up. "I need to cut him up first." She rummaged around some more, while saying, "But thankfully, I'm a nurse; I know exactly *how* to cut people up."

She came up with a bone saw, a hammer, and a chisel.

"Er, how long is this gonna take?" Isadora asked, as Sharday now climbed back into the bathtub.

"Not very long. I'm just gonna cut his head and limbs off his torso, trim them into smaller bits, and then break his torso into two or three pieces. That way we'll have no trouble moving them to the disposal site."

"Where *are* we going to dispose of his body anyway?" When Isadora asked this question, it struck her that she'd been pitifully naïve to prompt Sharday to kill Joe without even considering what to do about the body afterwards. "I was so thrilled that we were gonna get rid of him, that I never thought that far ahead."

Sharday looked up from cutting into Joe's neck with the scalpel. She paused the motion of the blade and blood spilled from the cut, which so far extended about halfway through the corpse's throat.

"Don't worry about it. I got the disposal place figured out."

Isadora sighed with relief. "Okay, so where?"

But Sharday didn't reply to the question. She was deep into the business of separating Joe's head from his body. Once she'd sliced the surface flesh open, her fingers roved deeper, still slicing away until Joe's head was held in place by just the neck vertebrae.

"Pass me the hammer and chisel," Sharday said.

Isadora hasted to comply. She watched, breathless, as Sharday placed the chisel against Joe's neck bones and then hammered away. The attacked vertebrae splintered. A few more slices with the scalpel and Sharday was holding out Joe's severed head to Isadora.

"Drop it in the bathtub behind me."

Isadora accepted the faceless head and then dropped it near Sharday's feet. Then she sat on the toilet seat and watched.

Sharday Brooks took Joe's corpse to pieces with such efficiency that Isadora wondered where she'd learnt such skill.

She's pulling him apart like he's a thanksgiving roast.

But pull Joe apart with expertise Sharday did. Thirty minutes after she'd begun, Joe Parker's corpse was in about twelve pieces and the bathtub was seemingly overflowing with blood and body fluids.

Sharday dropped her gruesome tools on the bathroom floor and sat down on the pieces of corpse, with her back against one end of the bathtub and her arms up on its edges.

"I'm fucking pooped from doing this," she groaned. "I feel like a just finished a triple shift at the clinic."

"I'll fetch you a beer," Isadora offered.

"Yeah, that'll do great," Sharday agreed. "But wash your hands and feet first before you step out into the corridor. You don't wanna leave DNA evidence for the cops to trace."

Isadora cleaned her hands and feet and then hurried over to the kitchen. She got two cold beers out of the fridge and hurried back.

Halfway back to the bathroom, she put the beer bottles down by the bedroom door, turned around, and walked back to the kitchen.

I might as well take along the garbage bags to pack the body parts in, she thought. *We'll need those for sure.*

CHAPTER 11

Aaron & Friends

Aaron Lee grinned to himself when he heard the car horn blare down in the parking lot outside his apartment building in downtown Springfield, MA.

He stepped out onto the apartment balcony and confirmed that his buddy Tom Wheatley (with whom he split the rent of the fourth-floor apartment), had arrived with their fellow travelers.

However, to his surprise, there were *two* vehicles downstairs: a white pickup truck was pulling up beside Tom's blue Lexus sedan.

Tom only went to pick up Bobbi and Erica. So, who else is coming with us on this impromptu trip?

Aaron waved down at Tom and the others as they spilled out of the two vehicles.

He now recognized the muscular black man and young Latina who were getting out of the pickup truck.

Oh, that's Bobbi and Erica's photographer friend Cedric, and Cedric's girl Rosa.

Down in the parking lot, Tom had his phone pressed to his ear. Aaron's cellphone rang a moment later.

"Bro, we can see you and you can see us," Tom said. "Get down here and let's hit the road."

Aaron watched Erica grab the cellphone from Tom's hand and add: "Yeah, get your slacker butt down here already."

"On my way," Aaron laughed and hung up.

After a look around the living room to ensure that he'd not forgotten anything essential, Aaron grabbed the last of the traveling cases he and Tom had packed for their trip and left their apartment.

A short while later, the blue Lexus and white GMC pickup pulled out from the parking lot and headed out of Springfield, east towards Raynham and an unplanned date with destiny.

***

Aaron Lee and Tom Wheatley had been roommates for three years. Outside of work (Aaron worked at Cashstretch supermarket, while Tom taught math at a local high school) the two did everything together.

This weekend the guys intended seducing best friends Erica Wells and Bobbi Kolinski together.

Just like Aaron and Tom were always together, so Erica and Bobbi were hardly ever apart from each other. The two young women even worked together; both were manicurists at the same nail salon, and they too shared an apartment.

In fact, the two ladies seemed to be so joined at the hip that Tom had once suggested to Aaron that they were lesbians and not worth pursuing romantically.

But the girls themselves had blown up that theory by suggesting a double date with the guys.

Which leads up to this weekend, Aaron thought in satisfaction. *Two days of nothing but seduction and relaxation and hopefully . . .* He laughed to himself . . . *lots of . . . fucktion.*

At the moment, Erica, who had a thing for Tom, was seated beside him and alternating between staring at the passing countryside, smiling coyly at Tom, and checking Instagram on her phone.

Bobbi, who similarly liked Aaron and was similarly seated beside him in the back, was similarly occupied with her cellphone, in her case checking the likes for she and Erica's YouTube fashion channel.

After a while Erica looked up from her phone. "We're doing okay," she told Bobbi. "These outfits we borrowed from your aunt are gonna be a hit with everyone." She flashed her flashily manicured nails. "Our competition is gonna die of envy."

"Yeah," Bobbi agreed, momentarily fingering the pendant dangling between her breasts. "I just hope the house vibe matches the clothes. They're rather gothic."

"Hey, guys," Erica said after a peek at her cellphone, "are you sure Billy's friends are gonna be okay with Rosa and Cedric also crashing their party?" She gestured back between the seats in the direction of the white pickup that was trailing them out of town.

"No problem," Aaron replied them. "Billy said the more the merrier."

"You sure they'd not just planning to murder us all?" Bobbi said with mock seriousness. "It's an odd invite to get so all-of-a-sudden."

Erica laughed. "Murder us? Bitch, you worry too much. Anyway, good thing that Rosa's a cop then." She punched Tom on the arm and laughed. "Hey, if either of you guys tries anything funny with us, it's on your own heads."

Bobbi laughed too, and said, "Rosa isn't a cop. She's still at the academy. She's not graduated yet. In fact, considering the amount of time she spends on social media, I doubt if she's ever gonna graduate and become a cop at all."

"Doesn't matter," Erica replied. "She's got a gun and we asked her to bring her gun along."

"Hey, I thought cadets aren't licensed to carry guns," Tom said.

"It's actually her mom's gun," Bobbi explained. "Rosa adopted the gun after her mom died."

"What do you two need a gun for?" Aaron asked in a worried voice. "Now I'm worried that you two crazy bitches are gonna shoot up everyone."

Erica laughed louder, now practically bouncing with amusement in her front seat. "No, silly, we want to use the gun as a prop for the fashion shoot. We already told Cedric what we've got in mind: sort of Lizzie Borden, but updated. Where she shoots people instead of axing them."

"But still, why invite so many people you don't really know?" Bobbi asked. She frowned at Erica. "I still think they're gonna slit our throats and drink our blood." She leaned back in her seat. "For your info—neither of us are virgins, so we'll be of no use in summoning Satan."

Erica rolled her eyes. "Now you've gone and ruined our surprise. I was hoping they'd find that out for themselves."

"Speak for yourself!" Bobbi countered with a laugh.

Aaron pretended he'd not heard their short exchange and concentrated on studying his cellphone.

This weekend is getting off to a flying start and we've not even begun drinking or getting stoned yet. Well, Tom at least is definitely getting laid this weekend.

"Okay, ladies," Tom said from the driver's seat after turning the BMW onto a side road. "No, we're not gonna sacrifice you. We're nice guys, not into that Satanist crap. Okay, according to Billy, they're trying to prove the house ain't haunted."

"Haunted? Ugh!" Bobbi said, wrinkling up her nose in horror. "You guys didn't mention *that* when you invited us along." She grimaced at Erica. "I thought this was gonna be a romantic getaway, not some creepy ghost hunt."

Erica grinned back at Bobbi with a mischievous twinkle in her blue eyes. "Actually, girl, Tom did tell *me* about the ghosts, but I neglected to tell *you* about them."

"Why the hell not?"

Erica laughed. "Because I know how much of a scaredy-cat you are. Telling you there might be ghosts in the house would've made you insist we not go there." Then Erica looked confused for a moment. "What I don't get tho', is, if you're so scared of supernatural stuff, why you wear that creepy pendant all the time."

"I like it," Bobbi said defensively, unconsciously fingering the pendant, which was black in color and shaped like an octopus, but a weird one that had a humanoid face and teeth in its middle. The necklace was also made entirely of one piece of material, with the cord that suspended it being the topmost set of octopus tentacles, which were much longer than the rest, long enough to extend around the wearer's neck. The necklace had no clasp; the wearer secured it by tying the thin ends of that topmost set of tentacles into a knot.

"I think it's a cute necklace," Bobbi went on. She turned to smile at Aaron. "Aaron, don't you agree my necklace is cute?"

Aaron, who had been smiling happily to himself ever since Bobbi had mentioned that she'd been looking forward to a 'romantic weekend,' nodded seriously. "It's very nice," he said. "Scary too tho'."

Bobbi pouted. "What do you mean, *scary?*"

Aaron tried to explain without reducing his chance of seeing her panties this weekend. As he was obviously expected to do now, he reached out a hand and lifted the pendant away from her breasts. "Well, it's very well-crafted jewelry, but . . ." After a fruitless search for anything better to say, he joked: "Okay, ask yourself this question: if your pendant came to life, would you want to be around it?"

Bobbi pondered on that for a few moments, then she leaned in close to Aaron and whispered throatily in his ear, "Agree with me that it's cute or else you'll be fucking your hand this weekend."

She was so close; the mingled smells of her perfume and her shampoo seemed close to intoxicating him. Aaron found it hard to control himself. His natural impulse was to turn his head and kiss Bobbi on the lips, to gaze blue eyes into gray eyes, and run his fingers through her long dark hair.

He hoped the hardened state of his penis wasn't obvious to Erica, who was watching them both with amusement.

Once Bobbi had removed her lips from nibbling his ear, Aaron coughed. "Well, actually guys, on further consideration, I mean, on second thoughts, I *love* this necklace that Bobbi's wearing. I love it so much in fact that once we return from this weekend trip, I'm gonna ask her to buy me one exactly like it."

"That's much better," Bobbi said, licking her lips at him.

"See, I told you he likes you back," Erica told Bobbi.

Aaron tried not to show his surprise on hearing this.

Hell yeah, I'm already in there! he thought with delight, just managing not to punch the air from sheer excitement.

He became aware that Bobbi was staring at him. Her eyes were a dark shade of gray and seemed to Aaron like long-awaited storm clouds about to pour rain on the parched earth of his heart.

"Anything wrong?" he asked her.

She nodded. "What's the scoop about the house? Why do they think it's haunted anyway?"

"To tell you the truth, I'm not sure," Aaron said honestly. "And I doubt Billy knows either."

"That is so vague it's frightening," Bobbi said. She leaned forward between the seats. "Hey, Tom, how 'bout you? Do you know anything else about where we're headed?"

Tom took his eyes off the road for a moment to glance back at her in the rearview mirror. "I do. After Billy told us about it, I did some research online."

"So . . . What did you find out? I mean, why do they think the place may be haunted?"

"From what I discovered, the building has a long history of folks vanishing there."

"What?" Bobbi shrieked and looked horrified. "Vanishing?" She looked at Erica and they both looked at Tom again.

"Vanishing?" Erica asked slowly. "You mean like, as in people going missing in the place?"

Tom shrugged. "From the online info, the building is like the Bermuda Triangle of houses. Folks move in, live there for a while, and then are never seen again."

"For real, bro?" Aaron felt impelled to ask. "Are you serious, or just having us on?"

"I'm dead serious. I'll share the webpages with you guys once we get there. If the web info is accurate—and I'm inclined to believe there's been a lot of embellishment to the stories—close to thirty persons have vanished at that house on Carver Street since the 1920s, when it was built."

"That's crazy," Erica said.

"Yeah, and we're driving over there," Bobbi added. "How suicidal we are."

"Don't start freaking out," Aaron told her, taking the opportunity to lay his hand on hers. "I'm sure it's not as bad as that. You know how folks are with all their creepypasta B.S."

He looked away from her for a moment and stared out of the rear windshield at the pickup truck behind them. Though he didn't really believe in the supernatural, Tom's information seemed to have cast an unpleasant shadow over their weekend.

"Is there anything else?" Erica asked Tom. "Anything else we should know?"

Tom drummed his fingers on the steering wheel. "One more thing: I don't know how true this is, but in the fifties and sixties the building supposedly belonged to a witch named Erin De Mornay, who was implicated, but never charged, in several occult murder cases that happened in Sacramento and Los Angeles."

"That's way across the country," Aaron pointed out. "How the hell did she get from here to there?"

"Yeah, or from there to here?" Erica added.

"Guys, I'm gonna give you all an ultimatum," Bobbi said while fingering her pendant. "Either we all stop talking about this spooky crap already . . . or you can just drop me off by the side of the highway and I'll call a Uber to take me back home."

Tom laughed. "Okay, no more talk about the Bermuda Triangle House we're headed to. No more talk of witches or human sacrifices either."

"Stop it!" Bobbi yelped. "I'm serious about not continuing this trip otherwise."

"Please stop it," Aaron pleaded. "Please, bro."

"Okay," Tom agreed. "But only because I know how much in love with her you are and I don't wanna ruin your chances."

"Tom, shut the fuckitty fuck up, or when we stop to buy gas, I'll get out of your damn car along with Bobbi and we'll both walk back home."

"No, we'll call a Uber," Bobbi told him, linking her fingers in his and squeezing.

"Yeah, we'll call a Uber," Aaron agreed with her, with a conspiratorial wink.

Erica giggled. "Ha ha ha. I can see what you two are up to back there. But, Tom, indulge them please."

"Okay," Tom said. "No more scary tales for the little boys and girls. We're just gonna drink and get stoned and maybe fuck and then . . . drink some more and hope the ghosts don't come on us when we're too intoxicated or exhausted to defend ourselves, and try to rip our heads off our bodies, and take—"

"SHUT UP, MAN!!!" everyone, Erica included, yelled at him.

CHAPTER 12

Paul, Jennifer, & Billy

Back at the house in Raynham, Phoenix Aurora seemed to have vanished for the time being.

The front door had a wide glass window in its upper half and opened into a short entrance hall.

The interior of the house was neat and clean. Paul, Jennifer, and Billy quickly made themselves at home.

After storing their groceries in the kitchen, they ascended the spiral staircase that linked the floors.

"There's a bedroom downstairs too," Paul pointed out when they reached the upper floor.

"How many bedrooms does this house have?" Jennifer asked.

Paul swung the ring of house keys on a finger. "Three, according to Marko. Two up and one down."

But, to their surprise, the house actually had four bedrooms upstairs, and when they all came downstairs again, they discovered that it had two lower bedrooms, not one.

"Well, the boss clearly got his facts wrong," Paul said, while scratching his head in some puzzlement. "His new house is bigger than he thought." He stared at Jennifer as they stood in the doorway of the larger of the two guest bedrooms. "His supposedly three-bedroom purchase actually has six bedrooms. Babe, how is that even possible?"

Jennifer shrugged back at him. "Simple. Your brother-in-law was clearly given the wrong specs by the realtors."

Paul looked at Billy, who nodded his agreement.

"I think she's right," Billy said. "According to what the housekeeper Phoenix Aurora said, people sort of shun this place, so maybe the realtors do too? If they're also scared by the legends, they'd hardly come in for a proper look. In that case, it's easy to mix up the house specs and stuff."

"Or," Jennifer added, "some previous tenants made some add-ons to the house and the realtors didn't update their building plans."

Paul nodded, though the incongruity still baffled him. His companions' explanations made perfect sense, but their sensible reasoning left him unsatisfied.

What's troubling me now? Oh, I get it. I feel as if the house is playing tricks on us, and I'm almost expecting that the next time we go upstairs, this building will have exactly the number of bedrooms advertised on the realtor's website: three, not six.

Paul laughed softly to himself. *Ghost bedrooms? Yeah, that's a new one! Ha ha ha ha! I must be crazy to even consider such a thing. Well, I'm sure Phoenix Aurora—I still can't get over how weird that name is; she must be into New Age astral shit or Wicca or whatever—I'm certain she'll have some sort of explanation when she comes back here.*

He became aware that his girlfriend was tugging on his sleeve.

"Yeah, babe?"

"So," Jennifer asked. "Are you guys ready to go to the liquor store now, or do you wanna postpone it till tomorrow?"

Paul thought a little. He felt a little disoriented by the house oddity, and felt he needed a drink tonight.

After checking the time on his watch, he said, "Yeah, let's go, babe. We're walking tho'. It's not too far down Broadway."

Jennifer looked at Billy, who shook his head.

"Nah, I'm too tired to do any walking tonight. Once you guys leave, I'm gonna go have a bath and watch some TV."

"Fair enough," Paul said. "See you when we get back."

On that note, he and Jennifer left the house and hit the road.

To Paul's strange relief, the night and the world outside of the building seemed welcoming around them.

CHAPTER 13

Isadora and Sharday

"Shit, we're not alone tonight," Sharday groaned.

From the passenger seat of Sharday's car, Isadora studied the man and woman who'd just stepped out of the driveway of the building they were headed for.

The pair turned left and headed up Carver Street, towards the Sunflower Motel and possibly Broadway.

"I thought you said it's an empty house?" Isadora told Sharday as Sharday pulled the car to the side of the road and parked. "So, what are *they* doing here?"

"It is an empty house," Sharday said. "I'm as perplexed as you are; this place has been empty for years."

"No mystery there then," Isadora said. "Someone either bought or rented it."

But Sharday shook her head at her. "No. No. No. Not this place. Nobody in their right mind in this county would buy this place. It's got a reputation of being haunted and cursed."

"Maybe someone from outside the county then?"

Isadora was about to say more, but Sharday tapped her on her arm.

"Come on," she said, "Let's walk over for a closer look."

They got out of the car and then hurried over to the driveway of the house, where they then ducked behind a tree and studied the building and its immediate environment.

It was a really old house.

A silver BMW was parked at the top of the long driveway, and, both upstairs and downstairs, some of the house lights were on.

"Well, someone's clearly home," Isadora said. "What are we gonna do now? We need to find another place to dispose of Joe." The thought of Joe's body, neatly packed into four doubled garbage bags, haunted her.

"No need to look for somewhere else," Sharday told her. "As we can both see, the house residents just stepped out for a walk, or maybe to buy something."

65

Isadora mused on this. "They didn't take their car. That means they won't be gone long."

"No, it means they *will* be gone long; longer than if they did take their car. You know this town as well as I do. There's nothing over that way except the motel, McDonald's and a couple other restaurants, and the church. So, if they went to buy anything other than dinner, it'll be down at that small shopping center on Broadway, which is at least a ten-minute walk either way."

To illustrate her point, Sharday gestured towards the top of the road, where, if Isadora squinted, she could just make out the walking couple, the man with his arm around the woman, making a right turn onto Broadway.

"See what I mean?" Sharday said. "They're headed for the shopping center." Sharday hugged Isadora tight. "Don't worry, hon. I'm figuring that they won't be back here for at least thirty minutes. They've gotta pick out their purchases from the shelves and pay for them too before heading back here."

Isadora shivered in the cold breeze. "I wish I shared your optimism. But . . . burying a corpse in the basement of an occupied building? Seems to me like . . . like we're courting disaster."

Sharday laughed. "Not here, we're not. You'll find out why once we're inside of it."

"What if someone else is home?" Isadora insisted. "They'll call the cops on us."

But Sharday shook her head and to Isadora's surprise, produced a small revolver from her jacket pocket. "No one will be calling anyone on us. Not, tonight; and if they become a pain in the ass, maybe not ever again."

The sight of the firearm shocked Isadora to her core. She stared at the weapon which glinted in the illumination of the nearby streetlight. She studied Sharday's face. In this darkness, the negress's face was almost unreadable, but Isadora could feel her girlfriend's desperate determination.

"I didn't know you had a gun on you," Isadora told her.

"Come on, let's do this," Sharday replied. "The longer we're indecisive, the more time we're wasting. Honey, I don't intend to shoot anyone, but . . . Listen, my main concern now is that that couple who moved into Hell House hasn't installed a security system yet. . . .

66

Or that, if they have, they forgot to reactivate it when they stepped out of the place."

Isadora followed Sharday back to the car, and a few minutes later, they returned to the cover of the trees beside the house. Each of them was carrying two bags full of Joe, and in addition, Sharday was carrying a crowbar. Both of them were wearing latex hospital gloves.

Isadora was surprised at how light her own bags of ex-boyfriend were, but Sharday had earlier explained he weighed less because they'd drained the blood out of him. And, of course, because they were each carrying only half of him.

The two women hurried through the trees to the east side of the building, where Sharday said the kitchen was situated.

All through this short trip, Isadora saw no sign of there being anyone in the house.

I hope there isn't, for their own sake, she thought.

Possibly because of its age, the house had no attached garage. This meant that its kitchen opened directly to the outside of the building.

"Okay, here we are," Sharday said, when they arrived beside the kitchen door.

Both women dropped their garbage bags of human remains on the grass, and studied the kitchen entrance. As expected, the door was shut. The kitchen lights were on but it seemed empty.

"Time to see if our luck is good," Sharday said, and then she turned from looking at the kitchen to address Isadora. "I'm going to jimmy the window open," she explained, while waving her crowbar in the air. "If the security alarm goes off, don't wait for me. Hightail it out of here—I'll be right behind you. We'll take Joe's remains back to your place, store him in the freezer and work out another means of—"

"The d-d-door j-j-just ope-ope-opened," Isadora stammered, stabbing her right index finger over Sharday's shoulder.

"What?"

Sharday turned back to look at the kitchen, and saw that it was true. The kitchen door was slowly swinging inward.

She looked back at Isadora. "Did you see what happened?"

Isadora nodded. "Yeah, I did. There still wasn't anyone in the kitchen, that much I'm certain of. But I heard a click and the kitchen door swung open."

Sharday mused on this. "You're sure there was no one there?"

Isadora nodded. "Hundred percent sure."

Sharday grinned at her. "It wasn't properly locked then. Our luck is in. If caught, we can't even be charged with breaking and entry, just with 'entry.'"

"I'm not so sure," Isadora said. "After what you just said about this place being cursed and haunted, I'm getting the feeling that the building opened its own door. Like it's expecting us; like it wants us to come inside it . . . For some bad reason."

Sharday looked from Isadora to the opened door and back at her again, and then laughed. "You watch too many horror movies. You should stick to chick flicks like I do."

"I'm not really liking this."

"You just killed a man, and now all of a sudden, you're scared of ghosts? Come on, the basement is waiting for us."

Sharday dropped her crowbar on the grass, picked up her two bags of Joe, and boldly made her way over to the kitchen door.

After a sigh of worry, Isadora picked up her own bags and followed her.

CHAPTER 14

Billy

Completely unaware that downstairs there were intruders entering the house, Billy Evans had just gotten through hanging up his clothes in the closet of his chosen bedroom.

Now dressed in a tee shirt and shorts that showed off his muscular young body to good effect, he left his bedroom (the rear one on the west side) to fix himself a sandwich in the kitchen.

Then it would be time for Netflix.

When Billy reached the stairs, however, he discovered that the hallway door situated almost opposite the stairs was now open.

Earlier, when he'd come upstairs along with Paul and Jennifer, the door had been shut. So now, Billy naturally walked over to the door to see who'd opened it.

The door opened onto a wide balcony that was semicircular in shape and was topped by a cupola.

Billy stepped outside and walked towards the balcony railing, noting as he did so that the floor was uneven. The balcony lights were turned off, but in the illumination from the hallway, he made out an arrangement of straight and curved grooves cut into the floor that apparently extended across the entire balcony.

Am I walking on the pentagram that's supposedly carved into the floor up here? he wondered.

There was no one outside here. Billy stood with his hands on the railing, staring out at the neighboring woods and the houses that dotted them.

"You're such a strong young man," a female voice whispered in his ear.

Billy tensed as he felt a body press against his from behind along with a concurrent smothering of his senses by heady gusts of perfume.

"Who? Who are you?" he gasped, beginning to turn around. But a soft female hand pushed his face in the opposite direction.

"Don't turn around. It's just me, Phoenix Aurora."

Billy tried to relax, but found it impossible.

69

"The housekeeper? Where the hell did you vanish to earlier?"

"It doesn't matter, does it?" she asked, pressing herself the more firmly against him, till he could feel her nipples poke him in the back. "I'm back with you now, that's what matters."

Billy felt his breath catch in his throat. "What do you want?" he gasped.

Phoenix Aurora laughed. "Surely you know what I want, pressing my naked body against yours."

She's naked?

Billy felt backwards with a hand and confirmed, that yes, Phoenix Aurora was bare-assed. He tried to slip a hand between their bodies but she pushed his hand away.

"No, let me satisfy you, Billy. I know it's been a long time for you."

"How can you know that?"

She laughed and slipped her right hand around Billy's body and into his shorts. He trembled when she grabbed his now-erect penis. "Billy, you're obviously a Man Going His Own Way."

"Yeah, that's true," Billy agreed. "I've had too many bad relationships with women. I'm looking after myself now."

"We're not all bad, you know." She'd freed his cock into the night air and begun tugging on him, while holding him firmly in place against the balcony railing. "Even if you're going your own way, every now and then you need a woman to take you firmly in hand." She kissed his right ear and then nibbled it delicately, while continuing to stroke him. "And I'm very good at lending a hand. Don't you agree?"

Her voice was like honey. Somehow, the honey seemed poisoned, but it was honey just the same.

"You lend the best hand I've ever had lent to me," Billy agreed as his legs tensed up and threatened to buckle beneath him. Her nipples felt hard as stones as she pressed him against the railing. He stared out over the darkened countryside, but hardly noticed it at all. "Oh shit, momma, I'm gonna come," he groaned.

"Let it out, baby. Give it to momma."

Her voice was an intimate instruction to let go of himself.

Billy let it out. Of recent he'd been practicing semen retention to boost his masculine energy, and he'd built up a major backlog of come. And now it flowed out of him like a river.

His legs went wobbly and he collapsed on the railing.

He felt Phoenix Aurora's body lying on his own, pressing him in place, her sensual fingers manipulating him until she'd completely drained him, his male essence dribbling over her fingers.

Then she kissed him gently on the neck. "You're taken care of for a while. I'll be seeing you later."

Billy sensed rather than heard her departing. One moment she was with him and the next moment he was alone with the night.

CHAPTER 15

Sharday and Isadora

Inside the house, Sharday and Isadora turned right, walked a short distance, and soon arrived at a door with a key in its lock. Sharday unlocked and opened the door and they descended a flight of steps.

At the bottom of the steps, Sharday flicked a switch on the wall and the basement filled up with light.

The basement was empty and was floored with stones that were arranged into a familiar occult symbol. The floor consisted of red, white and black flagstones arranged to form a pentagram.

"Wow," Isadora said, entranced by the kaleidoscope of stones despite her need to be gone from here by the time the new house occupants returned. She dropped her garbage bags and stepped into the pentagram for a closer look. "What is this stuff?"

Sharday walked over to the middle of the pentagram, which was a two-foot-wide black stone circle. "It's how we're gonna make Joe disappear for good."

Isadora gaped at her. "We're gonna magick him away?"

Sharday rolled her eyes. "No, honey, we're not. What makes you think that?"

Isadora gestured around them. "Duh? You're standing in a pentagram and talking about making my nightmare ex disappear. What else do you expect me to think?"

Sharday knelt down beside the black stone circle. "Come over here and give me a hand," she said.

When Isadora joined her, Sharday pointed to the edges of the stone circle, which Isadora now noticed was separate from the rest of the floor, being skillfully recessed into a gap in the rest of the stone arrangement.

"This part screws off," Sharday explained. "We just twist it anticlockwise. Dip your hands in the crack around the edges till you feel the fingerholds."

Intrigued now, Isadora did as she'd been told. Feeling around in the circle of space around the center stone quickly revealed four recesses that comfortably welcomed her fingers.

"Okay, I'm good," she told Sharday.

"Now we twist counterclockwise. Carefully, so you don't skin your knuckles."

Isadora twisted and the stone spun easily. It spun a quarter-circle and then popped up. Isadora and Sharday both stepped back and then the stone circle flipped upright and remained erect, revealing both that it was actually affixed to a metal mechanism, and that it had previously covered a panel with numbered buttons on it.

"What the hell is this?" Isadora asked.

"It's the entrance to a hole," Sharday explained.

"Hmm, like an underground cave?"

Sharday shook her head. "I'm not actually sure what is down there. I know what I was told, but it's hard to believe that's the facts."

"What are you talking about?"

Sharday sat down on the pentagram, using the popped up stone cover as a backrest. "As far as I know, this place—this damn house— once belonged to a coven of Satanists. And you know devil worshippers are notorious for sacrificing people—infants, vagrants, runaways—you name it, they've sacrificed them at some time or other. And of course, with such a high body count, you need somewhere to dispose of the bodies or else . . ." She gestured to the opening in the pentagram. "So that's where this comes in. Supposedly, it's a like a portable, reusable black hole."

Isadora laughed. "A portable black hole? That's crazy."

Sharday nodded. "I think it's crazy too. However, the Satanists claimed that that's what's down there. They claimed they found the 'hole' somewhere—I think they called the somewhere 'Alternity'— and then they tethered the hole here so they could use it to dispose of their sacrifice victims afterwards. But I don't believe in that supernatural crap. What I think happened is that there's some kinda natural fault line under the house that drops like forever, so if you dump things down there, they're too far down to retrieve. No traces of the corpse and *no smell* either." Sharday tapped the access panel. "One thing is certain, however. Whoever or whatever goes down there won't ever be seen again."

"I prefer your explanation too." Isadora grinned broadly. "Ha ha ha, this is just prefect. Even if the homeowners do meet us here after we've gotten rid of Joe's body, there's nothing to accuse us of. We'll just claim we lost our way."

After saying this, Isadora gestured at the panel over the 'hole,' and then pointed to the garbage bags on top of it. "So, what're you waiting for, baby?" Open it up and let's throw the garbage away."

Sharday tapped the access panel and groaned. "We've a small problem. I don't remember the passcode."

Isadora's eyes almost bugged out of her head when she heard this. "What?" she practically yelled. Then she calmed down and whispered, "What?"

Sharday nodded. "I stored it on my phone, but I've switched phones since then and thrown the old one away . . . I'd forgotten that."

Isadora felt like crying:

So close . . . so close and yet . . .

"Try six six six," she suggested when she calmed down. "That's universal devil worshippers' code."

Sharday laughed at that. "Trust me, that's not it. Just gimme a few minutes. I'm certain it'll come back to me."

Isadora sat down next to Sharday. "Tell me something, baby: how d'you know so much about this anyway? Do you make a habit of killing your girlfriends' exes?"

Sharday frowned. "That's not funny."

"It's very funny. Oh, alright, I don't mean it like that." Isadora kissed Sharday's aggrieved pout. "I'm curious tho'. Do tell."

Sharday looked embarrassed. "It's a family thing," she said.

" 'Family' as in, your family worship the devil? I thought most black folks preferred church."

Sharday smiled. "Not like that, silly. What I mean is that I have a cousin named Smokey and he introduced me to this place."

Isadora nodded with understanding. "Okay, so Smokey was a Satanist and he tried to bring you into the devil's fold?"

Sharday burst out laughing. "You'll understand better if you just listen. Listen, this is what—"

"Before you go on," Isadora interrupted with a gesture up the stairs, "shouldn't we shut the basement door? I mean, in case that couple return home."

Sharday shook her head. "No, we want to hear them return." Then after a look at her wristwatch, she added: "Besides we've still got a little time before they get back here."

"Okay, please go on with your story," Isadora said.

"Well, my cousin Smokey wasn't a Satanist, he was a gangbanger. He lived in Philly and was a drug dealer."

Isadora saw that Sharday was giving her an inquiring look and nodded that she understood that when used in this context, the term 'gangbanger' referred to a gang member and not to someone who participated in multiple-men-on-one-woman orgies.

Sharday went on: "So, one night I get a phone call from Smokey and it's an emergency. See, apparently Smokey and his friend Hey-Lo, another dealer, had gotten into a scrape with some Boston hoodlums working for a guy named Marko Velli or something like that, and Marko's people had shot up Hey-Lo pretty badly. Smokey and Hey-Lo didn't want to go to the ER, so Smokey was calling to ask if I could give Hey-Lo some first aid and also stitch him up a bit. I said, I'd do what I could and asked for the address. And it turned out to be this place."

"Wow. So did you help the guy?"

Sharday shook her head. "Hey-Lo died while I was walking down the basement steps." She laughed. "Actually, I think Smokey brought him here specifically because he knew the dude was a goner, and he didn't wanna be driving 'round town at night with a dead nigger in the trunk of his ride."

"Tonight, that sounds somewhat familiar; don't you think?"

"Shut up, darling, and let me finish,' Sharday said. "So anyway, that's how *I* discovered this place. Smokey told me that he and his friends had been using the hole for years to make their criminal rivals vanish. Me? I've never used it till now, honest."

Isadora nodded. The story fit the facts; though she wondered how Smokey and his friends had discovered this place in the first place, unless some of them were Satanists.

"Do you remember the code now?" she asked a little desperately.

Sharday gave her a look of mental anguish. "Almost. It's teasing me, skulking around the edges of my mind."

"Why not call your cousin Smokey?

"I can't. Smokey's dead. A drug deal gone toxic down south. The New Mexico cops are still searching for Smokey's head and his cojones."

"Cojones?"

"You know—his testicles."

Isadora whistled in stunned surprise. That painted a gruesome mental image indeed.

Then she looked around at their four bags of corpse meat.

"Keep thinking, baby," she said. "We gotta leave this place soon."

She settled down to wait.

CHAPTER 16

Paul & Jennifer meet . . .

Paul and Jennifer were still down on Broadway, standing outside of the liquor store with their bags of purchases. Wine and beer and some bottles of whiskey.

"O.K., we bought *a lot* of stuff," Paul said. "This stuff is heavy. Maybe we should've bought less."

"Maybe we should've brought the car after all," Jennifer said, looking up and down Broadway and then back at the liquor store. "I'm not looking forward to walking back to the house while carrying all of this."

Paul nodded. "I misjudged the distance to this place. I don't remember it being this far."

Jennifer looked pissed off. "It's not far if you're in a car."

"Don't bitch. I'll call us a Lyft."

But suddenly, Paul realized that Jennifer was staring past him and that she was no longer paying attention to him.

"What now?" he asked her, beginning to feel a little irritated. Then, when Jennifer neither replied him nor stopped looking behind him, he turned around to see what or who she was looking at.

"Duke?" he said in surprise on recognizing the tall and thin man who was walking towards them. The man had a broad smile on his bearded face and was accompanied by a petite woman with bright red hair.

"Hey, bro," Duke Higgins greeted Paul. The two men shook hands and then hugged. Paul and Duke went back a long way.

"Hey, Jenny," Duke said afterwards. "And I'd like you both to meet Katrina. She's an old girlfriend of mine."

"Hi," Katrina said. She had large eyes in a small face, and thin lips. Like Duke, she had lots of tattoos.

"You're the last motherfucker in the world I'd've expected to meet in Raynham tonight," Duke Higgins told Paul once the introductions were over.

"I'd say the same for you," Paul replied. "I heard you got put away over some bum shooting rap."

"Bum rap for sure," Duke agreed, his lips twisted in a grimace. "Some mob boss in Boston ordered a hit on a kid and the cops pinned it on me 'cos the kid owed Marko fifty large and I'd been leaning on him to pay up or I'd fix him." He grinned, revealing yellow teeth. "But they never found the murder weapon, 'cos I didn't have it, so my lawyer got me a retrial and I got out three days ago."

"That's a lucky break, man," Jennifer said. "Someone I know got thirty years for something like that and till date he still swears he knows nothing 'bout it."

Duke nodded. "Yeah, the justice system is fucked up. Nowadays, the damn pigs don't care who they lock up. Any excuse will do to get us hoods off of the streets and into the penitentiary."

"Duke, I already told you how they think," Katrina said. "The cops assume that if you ain't done something wrong this time around, you've definitely done something in the past that they missed arresting you for, or you're gonna do something in the future that they might miss arresting ya for. So it don't matter if they arrest you now; it just means they don't gotta worry if you escape an honest rap later."

Everyone laughed at that. Paul decided that he liked Katrina.

"So, what are you guys doing here in Raynham?" Paul asked Duke, as a passing truck showered them all with its headlights.

"Just passing through, bro," Duke replied, then he gestured vaguely up Broadway. "We checked into the Sunflower Motel and then decided to drive down here and buy some booze." He laughed. "After being in prison so long, I got a thirst on me like you wouldn't believe."

"We're having ourselves a fun road trip to celebrate Duke's release from the state pen," Katrina explained. "We ain't got any particular destination in mind; we're rolling from state to state."

Jennifer laughed. "At least you guys brought *your* car here. Paul and I were just about legging it back to the house."

Duke Higgins nodded from Jennifer to Paul. "What're you guys doing here in Raynham anyway?

So, Paul explained to Duke Higgins and Katrina Sanderson about Marko's supposedly haunted house.

***

78

"Ha ha ha!" Duke laughed once Paul got through telling his tale. "You can't make this shit up. Marko Velli—of all fucking people on God's fucking planet—bought a fucking haunted house."

"We don't know that it's haunted," Paul protested. "You know how I don't believe in the supernatural."

Duke laughed some more and clapped his hands. "Guys, I gotta see this place." He turned to Katrina. "Hey, girl, how 'bout if we join them and go do our proposed drinkin' over at Marko's haunted building?"

Paul watched Katrina weigh her options for a second or three. Then she nodded.

"Hell yeah, I'm game," she told he and Jennifer. "It sure beats watching a ball game or pro wrestling with Duke in our motel room. I'm in the mood to get laid tonight and Duke keeps scheduling our sex life around the fucking TV, like the world ceased to exist while he was in the penitentiary."

Duke looked a little pissed off at her outburst, but then he shrugged, grinned broadly, and said: "Well, since we're all agreed on getting drunk at Marko's haunted house, let's get ourselves some more beer, shall we?"

So they all turned back toward the liquor store.

"Hey, baby, did I ever tell you how Paulie here once saved my life?" Duke asked Katrina as they pushed their way through the entrance of the liquor store.

"He did?"

Duke held the door open till Jennifer and Paul had stepped into the store too. "Hell yeah, he did. It happened four years ago, up in Boston. "See, back then, I was working for this Chinese dude named Chang Lee . . ."

CHAPTER 17

The Perils Of Being A Mobster's Brother-In-Law

Four years ago Paul had been working in Boston Chinatown with a Chinese gangster named Chang Lee. Chang Lee was dealing drugs for one of the Macao triads and to ensure that he and Marko Velli remain on good terms, had requested that the kingpin's brother-in-law work for him.

Paul was against it from the get go, but Marko had insisted, and back then Paul was considering asking his brother-in-law to finance his proposed dry-cleaning business, so he'd agreed to work with Chang.

But unknown to anyone, Chang Lee had ripped off his Macao bosses. Instead of forwarding the Macao triad's heroin to their inland connections in Ohio as agreed, Chang was using it to set up his own supply network.

And then the Macao guys discovered what was going on and there was gonna be hell to pay.

Paul hadn't known a thing about it. He just handled Chang's books and collected his paycheck and tried to work out exactly how he was gonna convince Marko to loan him $150,000.

At that time, Duke Higgins was also working for Chang Lee. Duke was Chang's chauffeur and bodyguard.

It was at this time that Paul and Duke became fast friends.

On the fateful day in question, Paul's car had broken down, and he was meeting his sister Petra Velli for lunch, with the intention of asking her to put in a good word with her husband concerning his intended loan request.

So, Paul had thought of borrowing Chang's car instead. The boss was a genial fellow and very friendly with Paul. He'd not mind loaning his expensive Bentley to Paul, so long as he didn't have any appointments that required its use.

Once Chang confirmed that he had no outings scheduled for the next three hours, Paul had gotten the car keys from Duke and headed down to the underground parking lot.

But when Paul arrived in the parking lot, he'd had a really bad feeling about driving; just looking at Chang's car almost made him sick. So instead, he'd returned upstairs to the office, returned the car keys to Duke, and then he'd called a cab to take him to his lunch date with his sister.

What happened during Paul's absence from work was that . . .

Well, Froggy Hamlin, a drug runner for the Ohio guys, had come over to see Chang.

'Froggy' was called that because he had massive elastic-looking lips.

The Ohio guys had gotten wind of what had been going on, and (without first discussing it with the Macao guys) had decided to fix Chang Lee.

So, Froggy and a group of enforcers had driven over to Chang Lee's Chinatown office, roughed him up a little bit in there, and then bundled him into the trunk of Froggy's car to take him away for a lot more rough treatment, until he explained why their cross-country heroin shipments hadn't been reaching them.

Seeing as Duke Higgins was there in the office too, Duke got beaten up along with Chang, and was going to be taken away for additional rough treatment too.

Then, just as they were about leaving the underground parking lot, Froggy had decided that they might as well take Chang's car along also. Chang's Bentley Flying Spur Mulliner was worth over a quarter-million bucks.

Froggy suggested that they keep the car until Chang made good on their missing drug shipments.

"Or we can bury the motherfucker in it," he'd joked.

Now, the original plan was that, as Chang's chauffeur, Duke Higgins would drive his boss's car, going ahead with the gangsters following behind.

And Duke, battered and looking really the worse for wear, did indeed get into the Bentley.

But it was right then that Paul returned from his lunch date with Petra Velli.

And that afternoon, Paul was so distracted by thoughts of borrowing money, that instead of reentering the building by the more convenient front entrance that he'd left by, he walked in the long way, through its underground parking lot.

Which was Duke's good luck.

Now, Paul had no idea what was going on. He had no idea at all that his boss Chang was locked in the trunk of the silver SUV parked next to his Bentley.

He greeted Froggy, whom he knew to be one of Chang's 'business associates,' and was about walking past the Bentley to the elevator when he saw Duke behind the steering wheel of the car.

On seeing Duke in Chang's car, the strange premonition of disaster that Paul had earlier felt now returned to bug him again.

And so, inexplicably worried, he leaned in the car window.

"Listen, bro," he told Duke in an urgent whisper, "whatever the fuck else you do today, don't drive this car."

"What you talking 'bout?" Duke asked. It was dim in the parking lot, and so Paul didn't notice yet that he'd been roughed up.

Froggy watched their exchange with some impatience, but said nothing. To his mind, all he needed do if Duke gave the game away, was knock Paul out too and dump him in the Bentley's trunk. The more people to torture he had, the better.

"Just don't drive this car out of here today," Paul whispered to Duke. "And don't ask me how I know it, but it's gonna crash or something."

"Huh? You been drinking?"

"All I know for certain is that driving this damn Bentley anywhere today is gonna be the worst mistake you ever made in your life," Paul finished.

Duke actually began telling Paul to shut the fuck up, but then he saw something in Paul's eyes that convinced him the man was serious.

And so, Duke got out of the car (which was when Paul finally noticed that he had a cut lip and a black eye) and told Froggy, "Shit, man, I dunno what's wrong with my head, but I can't hardly see straight. My eyes keep crossing or something like that. I'm gonna have an accident if I drive."

Froggy shrugged. "Ride in my ride then, tough guy. I don't want you sitting beside or behind me while I'm concentrating on the road."

"Yeah, sure," Duke replied and after giving Paul a confused look, got into the Ohio guys' SUV.

And so, Froggy Hamlin climbed in behind the wheel of Chang's car, turned on the ignition, and was promptly drenched in concentrated acid.

The police later determined that some evil genius had tampered with the airbags on the driver's side of Chang Lee's Bentley, removing the original ones and replacing them with special acid-filled ones, and then rewiring the car so the airbags would deploy and explode on starting the ignition.

This seemed to have been done so that the vehicle's driver wouldn't be able to assist his passenger when the acid-filled reservoir that that same evil genius had installed in the ceiling of the car opened up and drenched the rear of the vehicle.

As it happened, the rear seat was completely dissolved away.

The modifications to the Bentley had to have been made overnight. Intended target: Chang Lee, who'd uncharacteristically spent the night in the office.

But since Chang hadn't gone anywhere that day . . .

Anyhow, that was the end of Froggy Hamlin. No one dared approach the vehicle to help him while he screamed and the flesh peeled off of his bones and his face dissolved into bloody jelly and his eyes popped and splattered the windshield with their contents.

Everyone watched Froggy melt away to bubbling slop.

After seeing that, those hardened Ohio gangsters, men who were used to bloody gunfights and breaking faces with brass knucks, and throwing corpses encased in barrels of cement into the Muskingum River, those hard men didn't even have the nerve to torture Chang Lee anymore. They'd lifted him out of the trunk of their car and flung him onto the garage floor. They'd kicked Duke out of their car like he was poisonous. Then they'd sped away like they were fleeing for their lives.

The rumor on the mob grapevine was that those Ohio guys hadn't stopped trembling with fear until they'd crossed the border into New York State.

What had apparently happened was a crisis of miscommunication. Just like the Ohio mobsters hadn't told the Macao guys of their plans to snatch and torture Chang Lee, so also the Macao triad hadn't informed the Ohio mob that they planned to wash Chang Lee out of this life with an acid bath.

Ironically, Chang Lee was still alive and well today, and was still dealing drugs in Boston. He however walked with a limp now, having broken his left hip when the gangsters had dropped him on the floor.

Now, however, Chang did what the Macao bosses told him to without reservation. He no longer messed with their heroin shipments to Ohio.

See, Chang Lee was the one who'd had to call the cops that day to come deal with Froggy's remains. Meaning he'd gotten a very good first-hand look at what disobedience to the Macao triads could result in; seeing as he'd clearly been the intended target of that acid bath and not Froggy Hamlin.

And that was why Duke Higgins owed Paul Dunford his life.

The day after that acid attack, Paul quit working for Chang Lee and went to ask Marko Velli for the $150,000 loan that had gotten him into his debt troubles.

CHAPTER 18

Billy's Nightmare

Back at the house, Billy was still up on the second-floor balcony.

Billy felt nicely relaxed, so relaxed in fact that he'd not yet tucked his manhood back into his shorts.

The moon was out, but even though it was over on the other side of the house, its rays gave the backyard trees a softened, comforting appearance. The wind was cool, but not so much that Billy needed to go inside.

Billy smiled to himself.

Yeah, sure, the lady ruined my semen retention routine, but it was more than worth it.

He gave himself a thumbs up.

And I think she wants to go again later too!

Suddenly, however, Billy felt like he'd somehow slipped into a nightmare. He was awake and yet not exactly awake. But he wasn't asleep either.

There on the upper balcony, Billy Evans watched a group of five men drag three naked and bound young girls out here onto this same semicircular balcony and then proceed to sexually abuse them with knives.

Billy tried to move, but his range of motion was limited to waving his arms. He tried to protest what he was seeing, but his tongue was frozen in his mouth.

Nor could he close his eyes, or even turn them away from the horror nearby.

The trio of female victims were unable to plead for mercy—their tongues had been cut out. The girls couldn't beg for mercy and no mercy was shown to them. They were sexually penetrated with the knives over and over again, so that they bled out onto the balcony.

The abuse was happening inside the pentagram carved into the balcony floor, and the blood of the terrified young victims drained into the lines of the pentagram and flowed to the pentagram's center, where, as impossible as that should be, the blood flowed *upward* over the body of a young woman sitting there, a woman whose face and body showed the ravages of extreme drug abuse.

The young drug addict was masturbating with the three victims' severed tongues. She was also chanting something under her breath, her lips and tongue moving silently, her bad teeth glaringly obvious each time she pronounced certain words. Each time she reached orgasm with one of the victim's tongues, she stuffed it up inside her vagina and resumed pleasuring herself with another one.

Yes, their blood flowed *up* and over her, and then, at some point, it seemed to sink into her body.

To Billy's unwilling gaze, it looked like the drug addict's skin absorbed the three teens' spilled blood in the same way that sand soaks up water.

Two of the teens quickly died from sexual blood loss. The third girl, who survived the knife-rape, was then dispatched after her sisters with a stab to the throat that was so brutal, the blade went all of the way through her neck.

While laughing, the man who killed her pushed the ritual dagger down right to the base of its grip, and then he left her like that, with that strangely curved and rune-engraved blade stuck through her neck, and snorted a line of cocaine from a silver mirror, while she gurgled and then finally choked on whatever pathetic sanguine reserves still flowed through her veins.

Billy saw this as if he was there, but when he reached out to touch the world he saw, he understood that it no longer existed. He was staring into the past, and the past was dead, the atrocity he was witnessing long gone.

The rape and murder of the three young women ended.

But the past didn't end there. Suddenly, Billy could see back through time, and what he saw was layer upon layer of stacked atrocities (many of them much worse than what he'd just witnessed), crimes committed within the walls and boundaries of this building that extended all the way back to when this house had been built.

Built and dedicated to the devil's work, Billy thought, with a feeling of intense nausea.

But no, this isn't just the result of a group of crazed Satanists who'd dedicated a building to the worship of their infernal master. There's something more about this building. Something buried deep in the past; a secret that almost no one who comes here even suspects.

People come here, they live here, and often they die here. But this house, this building has an impossible and a terrifying secret . . .

And then, the haze that had overcome Billy Evans's senses faded, the horrifying images faded also, and suddenly he was himself again.

What the hell was that about? he asked, as unreality became reality and that reality was the fact that he was standing by the railing of the balcony with his dick dangling from his shorts and his come splattered on the floor.

That was truly the best handjob I've ever had! Billy thought and pulled his shorts up.

But what the hell was that stuff I just hallucinated about those three murdered girls? O-fucking-K., I get it: the power of suggestion is working on me. What just happened was, I created my own mental dramatization of Phoenix Aurora's history of this house's brutal past. I don't know how I did that—nothing like this has ever happened to me before—but that has got to be what I just experienced. It's the only explanation that makes sense.

Billy told himself this, but yet found it hard to dispel a creepy feeling that now attached itself to him; the feeling that the house had wanted him to see what he'd seen; that the house itself was the agency that had created his nightmarish vision.

Preoccupied and bothered, he hurried off the balcony and headed downstairs.

CHAPTER 19

Isadora & Sharday

Down in the basement, Isadora was pacing about restively.

"I still can't believe you forgot the most important detail of all," Isadora said, pointing over to the 'almost-open' hole in the middle of the stone pentagram. "You planned everything else to absolute perfection and yet . . ."

Her agitated trudging had carried her over to the basement stairs. She sat down on the bottom step and waved her fingers at Sharday, who sat motionless against the stone lid, tapping her fingernails on the kaleidoscope floor.

"Hey, there!" Isadora called out. "Earth to Sharship! Earth to Sharship! Come out of your trance, biatch, or we'll both be going to jail!"

Sharday didn't reply or acknowledge Isadora's warning. Isadora began to worry again:

If Shar keeps looking straight ahead at those garbage bags we stuffed Joe into, we're screwed. If she can't remember the password, let's just get out of here. We'll leave Joe in my freezer like she suggested and think of somewhere else to let him rest in pieces. It seems so sad tho'—this hole in here would be perfect, if she could just remember those numbers.

"Shar, I got a question for you?" Isadora said after a while.

At first Sharday's introspection continued unabated.

"Shar, there's something I don't understand," Isadora persisted.

This time her words broke through Sharday's wall of concentration.

She waited until she had her girlfriend's full attention before going on: "If you knew we were coming here, why did you make us go to so much trouble to destroy Joe's face, his teeth, and his fingerprints?"

Sharday smiled. "I wanted to make Joe really suffer for hurting you the way he did. Just look at you: honey, you're so busted up, you're like a walking advert for legalizing manslaughter." But then she shrugged and looked serious. "But also, I had us do it in case something like *this* happened. Imagine if we brought your ex here as he was back at your place, and we found ourselves in this same situation; where would we start from?"

Isadora agreed that she made a good point.

Yeah, it's better to have something and not need it, than to need it and not have it.

And then Sharday grinned.

"Oh, I remember the damn passcode now," she announced.

Hearing that, Isadora sighed with relief. It literally felt like a huge weight had just been lifted off of her chest. "Great. What is it?"

"I don't remember," Sharday said.

Isadora gaped at her. "Huh? But you just said . . ."

"Don't freak out. I remember it's the year that Lulu Moorcock murdered her family here. That's what Smokey told me."

"Who's Lulu Moorcock?"

"A pornstar that our grandparents jacked off to."

"So . . . What year was it?"

"*That's* the part I don't remember. Gimme a minute to check online."

Sharday raised a finger for silence and then, while Isadora impatiently tapped her foot on the floor, googled the date.

"1976," Sharday finally announced.

Without further ado, she entered the four numbers into the numeric keypad on the metal cover to the hole and then hit 'Enter.'

From her seat on the bottom step, Isadora watched the metal internal covering that now formed the middle of the pentagram silently split into two halves that slid away out of sight beneath the floor.

She got to her feet and walked over to stare at the hole. Sharday also got to her feet.

Both women peered down into a foot-and-a-half-wide portal of darkness. Illogical as the feeling was, Isadora suddenly believed that this 'hole' really might descend forever, into an alternate reality, even.

"Wow!" she gasped finally.

"This gives me intense vertigo," Sharday said nervously. "I feel like I'm standing on the roof of a skyscraper, and the roof lacks a railing."

"I totally agree with you." Then a question occurred to Isadora. "How do they power this thing?" she asked, pointing at the hole. "I'm talking about the cover: does it only work when the building has electricity?"

While speaking Isadora was instinctively backing away from the impossible hole in the ground. The hole worried her no end; staring down into it made her feel queasy.

That her retreat finally brought her heels in contact with one of the garbage bags they'd come here to dispose of wasn't much of a relief.

"You know, I wondered about that too," Sharday replied her question. "Smokey said the Satanists connected it to some solar panels up on the roof, so that it works even when there's no electricity in the house." She stepped over to Isadora's side and tapped her arm. "Alright, enough daydreaming here. Let's do what we came here for and split. I'm certain we're on borrowed time already."

Isadora nodded her agreement and picked up the garbage bag by her foot. Suddenly nervous, she carried it over to the hole, positioned it carefully over the opening, and let go.

She grinned as inch by inch, the plastic bag slipped through the opening and fell out of sight. The hole may have assisted the bag's descent with a slight suction effect, but Isadora couldn't be sure of that. She watched the bag descend out of sight and then she listened to see if she would hear it striking bottom. But she heard nothing.

It really is bottomless, she thought. *I'd better not get too close to it.*

"Get out of the way!" Sharday called out from behind her. "I got toxic masculinity to dispose of too."

Isadora edged back. "Well, bye bye, Joe," she waved at the hole. Then she turned around to fetch her own second bag of ex-boyfriend.

CHAPTER 20

Billy meets Isadora & Sharday

On his way to the kitchen, Billy discovered that the basement door was standing open.

Thinking that the sexy housekeeper might be down there, he decided to investigate.

"Hey, Phoenix, you down here!?" he called out as he descended the basement steps.

Then, reaching the bottom of the steps, he paused and stared at the two women, one black and one white, in the basement. The black woman, who had short blonde hair, was standing off to one side and seemed about to pick up a stuffed garbage bag, while the white woman, who was an actual blonde, was carrying a similarly stuffed black bag towards a hole in the middle of the floor.

Something about that hole immediately bothered Billy. A hole seemed a weird thing to encounter in a basement, which was itself situated underneath a house.

Aaron's party must've arrived while I was em . . . 'busy' with Phoenix on the balcony; that's why I didn't hear their cars pull up. These ladies must be the two female friends that they mentioned. But are they dumping trash or what?

"I'm Billy," he said. "I've been expecting you guys. Hey, where are Aaron and Tommy? I was busy upstairs and didn't hear you arrive."

Since stepping into the basement Billy had wondered why these two women, whom he admittedly didn't know, looked so bothered. Surely, if they were Aaron's friends, they'd have an idea of who he was.

The white woman (who had a puffy battered face, with a black eye) looked particularly scared. So scared in fact, that she accidentally scraped her garbage bag against the side of the upright lid of the basement hole they were dumping their trash into.

The hole cover must've had a sharp projection along its edge, because all of a sudden, as the blonde jerked the bag away from it, the bag ripped open from top to bottom and several large reddish objects spilled out of it onto the floor.

It took Billy a few moments to understand that he was looking at a faceless human head, a pile of intestines, and a human arm, amongst other things. The fact that all of these human body parts dripped with blood assured Billy that they were recent creations.

What the hell? These two women aren't part of Aaron's party!

Billy turned to look at the negress, and discovered that she'd sidled up to him while his attention was distracted by the human body parts on the floor.

The black woman was pointing a revolver at him.

"If you dare move a muscle, you know what happens next," she told him.

Billy instinctively put his arms up. Only after doing so did it occur to him that she'd just warned him not to move.

"Who are you two?" he asked.

The women didn't answer. Instead, the black one looked at the white one. "Oops, Dora, we're busted," she told the blonde. "It never occurred to us to make certain there was no one else at home."

Billy couldn't tell what the blonde—Dora, right?—was more aggrieved by, the fact that he'd stumbled in on their gruesome murder cover-up/body-disposal activity—because, what else could they be doing throwing pieces of someone down a hole in someone else's basement—or that the garbage bag had burst and made a mess that she'd now need to clean up. She was gazing down at the spilled body parts like she dreaded picking them up.

Her black companion showed no sign of any such nerves.

The black woman looked coldly determined.

Billy studied her white friend's face in more detail. In addition to a black eye and a swollen and cut lip, the blonde had a livid bruise on the left side of her jaw, and also a long cut down the side of her nose.

She looked like she'd recently been beaten up.

Billy quickly put two and two together, and realized that the blonde had most likely been beaten up by the guy they were trying to dispose of. Then her African-American friend had intervened and . . . bye-bye, brutal bad boyfriend.

"What are we gonna do now?" Dora asked the black woman.

"We'll do what we earlier agreed," she replied. "We can't afford to leave any witnesses. You know that."

Billy didn't like the sound of that at all and decided to address the two women.

"Listen, ladies, this isn't any of my business," he said, lowering his arms while doing so. "How about if we all forget that I saw anything? I don't know anything about you both. I never saw either of you before. Besides you're both wearing gloves, so no fingerprints. Hey, listen, this isn't my house either, so if you just leave, it'll be the same as if you were never here."

The blonde looked like she was considering his proposal.

"Hey, Shar, what d'you think? We let him go or not?" The blonde giggled. "You know, he is kinda cute. I don't think he'll tell anyone about us."

But 'Shar' shook her head.

"Sorry, man," she told Billy. "But we can't let you leave. It's too damn dangerous. I ain't 'bout to be the cellblock bitch, just 'cos Dora likes your muscles and your baby blue eyes." She gestured to the hole in the middle of the room. "So, we'll dump you in there too and no one will ever find you."

"C'mon, gimme a break!" Billy protested. "I don't even know you two."

"You know our names. Just in case you missed them, I'll make a proper introduction. I'm Sharday Brooks and li'l mizz ditzy here is my girlfriend Isadora Grant. And—" here she indicated the spilled human remains on the floor "—we just got through killing her no-good piece-of-shit boyfriend Joe Parker and now we're disposing of his body."

Billy winced as Sharday prodded him in the gut with the revolver.

"Please, you can't do this to me!" he protested.

Where the hell have Paul and Jennifer gotten to? he wondered in horror. *If they don't get back here soon, I'm dead meat!*

He thought that Paul might have a gun with him too, but he wasn't sure.

And then, everyone in the basement was startled by a loud noise. It took Billy a few moments to understand that his cellphone was ringing in the pocket of his shorts.

Isadora fished in his shorts and got out the cellphone.

"It's some guy named Aaron," she told Sharday.

"Dump it in the hole," Sharday told her. "Aaron's the person he thought we were with."

"Stop!" Billy protested as Isadora walked over to the hole and dropped his cellphone down into it.

He waited, expecting to hear the sound of the phone striking bottom somewhere, but the anticipated noise was absent; as if the hole in the floor continued forever.

"I still can't get over how deep this thing is," Isadora said as she turned around. "It really does seem bottomless."

Sharday nudged Billy with the gun. "Now, Mr. Handsome, get moving. It's your turn to find out how deep that hole is—'cos we sure as hell don't know."

"Send us a postcard from hell, or wherever it ends," Isadora told him.

Dammit, I forgot! Billy thought as at gunpoint he was forced closer to the hole in the floor. *Phoenix Aurora is also in the house! She can help me out of this predicament! But how do I safely summon her? If I yell out, these two crazy bitches will most likely shoot me. But if I don't let Phoenix know there are intruders in the house, she may walk down here just like I did and also become their captive.*

CHAPTER 21

Aaron, Tom, Bobbi, & Erica

"No response," Aaron said and lowered his cellphone from his ear.

"Ah, I'm certain Billy's asleep or something," Tom said from the front seat.

"Or maybe, he's taking a crap," Erica added and burst out laughing.

"We'll soon find out anyway," Tom added. "We'll soon be in Raynham."

Aaron looked out at the passing Massachusetts countryside and nodded. Darkness lay heavy on the roadside woods now and he kept imagining he saw strange shadows out there, lurking between the trees or sitting on their branches.

What's the matter with me? he pondered. *I'm not normally as nervy as this. Okay, maybe Tom and Erica are right and Billy's elsewise occupied at the moment, but somehow, I get the feeling that we're heading into an unpleasant situation. Unfortunately for me, such an irrational feeling ain't something I can use as a sensible excuse to cancel the weekend trip that I personally planned.*

So, Aaron said nothing.

Instead, he twisted around and peered through the rear windshield at the white GMC pickup truck following behind them. Cedric had one hand on the truck's steering wheel while the other hand held a soda can to his mouth.

Aaron laughed; the black guy almost seemed a part of the night himself.

Rosa was saying something to Cedric, but then she noticed Aaron staring back at them, and waved to him.

Aaron was suddenly very pleased that Rosa had brought her gun along on this trip. He waved back at her and turned away from the rear window to stare instead at Bobbi. Bobbi was focused on her phone, and he could see that she was scrolling down the comments for one of she and Erica's recent fashion posts, this one showing them both made up as vampires.

Aaron almost looked away then; the vampire motif was a little too close to his recent feelings of disquiet about phantom things cavorting amongst the roadside trees. But then his attention was again drawn to the pendant Bobbi had on; the black octopus-like thing with a wolfish face and horrible jaws.

For a brief instant, the weird pendant struck him as the devil's confirmation of his worries. But then, Aaron shrugged off the weird vibe.

"I don't get it," he told Bobbi to make conversation. "Like Erica was saying earlier, if you're scared of ghosts and stuff like that, why d'you like this necklace so much?"

Bobbi was laughing at a fan's comment when he asked the question, but still, she put her phone aside and turned to him.

"You mean this thing?" she asked, the ghost of a smile dancing on her lips.

Aaron nodded. "Yep, What's the story behind the necklace?"

Bobbi peered down at the odd pendant and fingered it. "I lucked onto it by accident at an online auction."

"EBay?"

"No, not them. This was a goth place. A couple months ago, Erica and I wanted to rent some outfits for a fashion shoot and we found this obscure website . . . hey, Erica, what was the name of the website again?"

Erica was drinking an iced tea bought back at the convenience store where they'd stopped to buy gas. "Pentagrimmcouture.com."

"Yep," Bobbi agreed. "We didn't find any good goth outfits there, but they had an auction section where folks could sell antique stuff, and we looked through the antique jewelry they had on offer and I found this necklace."

"It's supposed to have belonged to a witch," Erica said. "I don't recall her name tho'."

"Erin De Mornay," Bobbi said with a smile. "She was supposed to be the real deal too—black masses and human sacrifices, and all that kinda evil shit. She apparently made the FBI's 'Most Wanted' list a few times too." Bobbi's facial expression now turned reflective. "I gotta admit it's kinda odd tho'—I mean, my fascination with this pendant of hers—'cos I'm not really into the goth and witchcraft thing at all. Neither of us is: Erica and I just dabble into different cultural subgenres and try to put together a fashionable look from each one for our fans."

"Right now, we just happen to be doing the horror genre," Erica said. "In a couple months we plan to move on to Old Wild West stuff—cowboys and Indians—those kinda outfits."

"Then we got the kinky sex-fetish shoots scheduled for the end of—"

"I'm sorry to interrupt you ladies," Aaron said. "But you said the necklace belonged to Erin De Mornay, right?"

Bobbi nodded. "Yeah, that's right. Why?"

Aaron felt very confused by the premonitions he felt he was having. "Tom, buddy, didn't you say earlier that the house we're headed for once belonged to a witch named Erin De Mornay?"

Tom laughed. "Yep, that's right. According to what I read up this afternoon, Ms. De Mornay owned the place during the fifties and sixties, or was it the sixties and seventies, or just one of those decades? I don't really remember, but it was somewhere about those times."

"Fuck," Bobbi said. "I didn't know that. We're going to *her* house?"

"Yep," Tom confirmed. "That we are."

Erica said, "I heard Tom mention her name earlier, but it didn't ring any bells with me. Like I told you guys, I didn't remember her name."

Bobbi gave Aaron a worried look. "What bothers me now, is how *I* didn't make any mental connection between her and the necklace when Tom said it. I must've zoned out or something. That would make sense if I was stoned, but not when we're having a sober conversation."

Aaron asked her: "You're serious about this, that you didn't hear what he said?"

She shook her head. "I'm certain I didn't, because I was paying attention to what he was saying. Remember how scared I got? So I'm sure—"

"Hey, you two, lighten up!" Erica said angrily. "Don't start getting the heebie-jeebies again! Bobbi, you're not gonna ruin our weekend, okay?" She twisted around between the front seats and gave Bobbi a searching gaze. "Okay?"

Bobbi sighed. "Okay, but remember it wasn't me who described that house as the Bermuda Triangle of houses. It was Tom."

"Aw, come on, everyone," Tom said with a broad gesture out of the car window at the town they'd just arrived in. "Lookee here, folks, we're already in Franklin, meaning we'll be arriving in Raynham in ten minutes max." He laughed. "And for everyone's info, according to the internet, Erin De Mornay died in the seventies. It ain't like she's over at the house with Anton LaVey waiting to sacrifice us to El Diablo. So, what're you both worrying about? Hey, hey, guys! Let's just have fun this weekend!"

"Hey, I've a great idea," Erica said. "Bobbi, if you're so worried about the necklace's ownership, throw it out the window." She grinned. "Problem instantly solved."

But Bobbi shook her head and tightened her grip protectively around the black pendant. "Uh uh. It cost me too much. You know that."

Erica nodded and grinned at both guys in the car. "Yeah, it did. $666.66 'cos the damn thing is supposed to have specific powers that no one could explain to Bobbi." Then she focused her attention on her friend again and giggled. "You know, girl," she said, "I've begun hoping that we do encounter a ghost or a reincarnated witch. Just imagine what that'll do for our fashion show channel in terms of likes, if we can catch it on film."

Bobbi sighed. "You won't let up on this, wilya?"

Erica laughed. "Not unless you do. C'mon, let's have fun this weekend, huh?"

Bobbi turned to look at Aaron. "What do you think?" she asked him.

He reached out and covered her hand with his again. "I guess it can't hurt. We're already here, so . . ."

"Okay," Bobbi agreed with a broad smile. "Let's have fun this weekend. Let's get drunk, get high and par-tee!" After making seductive eyes at Aaron, she added: "But, Tom . . . ?"

"Yeah?"

"I want a photograph of Erin De Mornay. First sight of her over there and I'm out of there like Speedy Gonzales."

Everyone laughed at that, Even Aaron, who was beginning to think that this pleasure trip of theirs might unfortunately turn into something unfunny.

CHAPTER 22

Billy, Isadora, & Sharday

"Okay, man, down into the hole you go. Jump in yourself."

Billy stared down at the hole in the basement floor and then at Sharday and then back down at the hole.

Staring at the hole in the floor brought his upstairs vision back to mind, mainly because he now understood that the colored stones that comprised the basement floor were arranged in the shape of a pentagram, and that the hole he was staring into was in the exact center of that pentagram.

Almost like this building is some kinda evil deity and I'm about to be sacrificed to it.

"Go on, jump in!" Sharday insisted.

Billy stared at her like she was nuts. "Are you fucking serious?"

"Yes," Isadora replied. "If you commit suicide, we won't kill you."

Billy revised his view of Isadora Grant being the innocent victim that her battered face had previously suggested she was.

I think she's really one of those masochistic passive-aggressive bitches who bully a guy until he erupts and beats them up, and then plays the victim card afterwards.

"I'm not going down there," Billy told Sharday angrily and took two steps backward. "What the hell do you take me for? Crazy?"

In response to his outburst, Sharday placed the gun against his right temple. "Motherfucker, you're going down into that hole, one way or another."

Isadora, meanwhile, was studiously looking Billy up and down.

"He's very well-built," she said finally. "He must work out a lot."

Her out-of-left-field remark surprised Billy.

What?

The weird remark clearly surprised Sharday too, and she growled at her girlfriend: "What the hell are you talking about? What does the boy's physical fitness have to do with this?" Sharday rolled her eyes. "Hey, hey, don't tell me you're already sizing up another man to beat your blonde ass up."

Isadora shook her head. "No, I don't wanna fuck him. It's just that . . . well, his shoulders are too wide. I don't think he's gonna *fit* into the hole."

Sharday glanced at the hole, then she looked back at Billy, and measured his shoulders with her eyes. "Oh shit, you're right. He won't fit through the opening."

Billy felt like he'd just been granted a new lease on life. But then Isadora said:

"But that's easy to fix. We just need to cut his arms off at the shoulders. The rest of him will go into the hole easy."

Sharday laughed, while Billy felt like he was in the middle of another nightmare. What they were suggesting seemed just as bad as his earlier hallucination of the cultists raping those poor teenagers with knives.

Cut my arms off? What the hell are these two crazy women tripping on?

Were it not for the gun aimed at his head, Billy knew he'd easily make mincemeat of these two bitches at once, but the gun made this impossible.

Sharday struck him as having an itchy trigger-finger. He suspected that she was mere moments away from shooting him. He wondered why she hadn't yet shot him.

"Wait here," Isadora told Sharday. "I'll go look for an axe or something."

Sharday nodded. "Check in the kitchen first. I think I saw an electric knife on the counter on our way in. Too bad I left my tools back at your place."

It was at that moment that Billy realized *why* his two captors hadn't shot him yet.

It's because they don't want a gunshot to possibly alert the neighbors, or Paul and Jenny when they return. So . . . so they ain't gonna shoot me except as a last resort. But . . . but if they realize they can do so after shutting the basement door, I'm screwed.

And, seeing as they're going to kill me anyway, I've nothing to lose by making a last-ditch attempt to save myself.

Since realizing that toppling Billy into the hole in one piece was out of the question, Sharday had stepped away from him. Though she still had the gun trained on him, her stance was more relaxed, like she realized she could shoot him dead before he either reached her or fled up the steps.

But, Isadora now made the error of walking between Sharday and Billy on her way to the steps.

Billy reacted the moment that Isadora's body had eclipsed Sharday's. He leapt forward, grabbed firm hold of the blonde woman, and, before shock could even register on her battered face, he launched her directly at Sharday.

Isadora knocked Sharday over and both women crashed down on top of the hole.

Neither of them went through it, but the mere realization of where they'd fallen was sufficient to disorient and scare them.

Jarred loose of her grip by the impact with the floor, Sharday's gun had dropped a short distance from her hand. Billy contemplated going for the gun, but Sharday snatched up the firearm again the moment he stepped towards the fallen women.

"Shit, he's getting away!" she said and attempted to roll Isadora off of herself so that she could see him.

"Hey, careful or you'll push me into the hole!" Isadora yelped, and scrambled back on top of her.

Billy decided there was no point tempting fate. He made himself scarce while they sorted themselves out.

And at the top of the stairs, he made sure to lock the basement door on the two women.

CHAPTER 23

Billy . . .

Safe for the time being with the basement door locked, Billy thought on what to do.

The most obvious and logical thing to do was to call for help.

But, his phone was gone, and, down there in the basement, Sharday and Isadora had a gun with them. He doubted that it would be long before Sharday shot off the lock.

Billy considered going upstairs to search for Paul's own gun.

But what if I'm mistaken and Paul didn't actually bring a gun with him?

Because, come to think of it, who in their right mind would dare break into Marko Velli's house . . . except possibly, two crazy women trying to hide a corpse. And what the hell was that hole in the basement floor? It seemed bottomless.

The other option was to try the landline in the living room.

But if it isn't connected, I'll be wasting valuable time—time that those two crazy women won't be wasting. And what if it is connected, but they break out of the basement while I'm on the phone calling for help, 'cos for one thing, I don't know the house number of this place . . .

After a glance towards the spiral stairway that linked the floors, Billy made up his mind.

I'll get out of here and ask for help in the house across the street.

Billy headed for the kitchen door simply because it was closer. The door was two yards to his left and he knew that it opened direct to the outside and not into a garage, which would have created an additional distance to traverse before he'd be safely outside of the house.

The important thing now is to get outside the house. Down there in the basement, Dora and Sharday can't possibly know which way I went!

So, Billy hurried into the kitchen. The kitchen door stood wide open mere steps away, but Billy discovered that try as he might, he couldn't reach the door. The harder he tried to reach it, the further away from him it seemed to get, and yet, the kitchen was still exactly the same size, and nothing inside of it (not even the clearly distant door, apparently) had altered their positions.

What's going on? Billy wondered in a panic, doing his best to reach the door that was right in front of him. *It's like I'm on a treadmill! Like I'm running in place!*

A bead of sweat ran down his forehead when he remembered that at any moment now, Isadora and Sharday might break out of the basement.

And since they intend to chop me up, they may have no reservations about shooting me now!

Indeed, he saw the electric knife that the negress had mentioned lying on the kitchen counter.

The sight made him redouble his efforts. But he seemed to be running in a dream, once more stuck inside of a vision.

Billy was doing his utmost not to panic at the impossible situation he'd become trapped in, but still, he almost leapt out of his skin when he felt a hand touch his shoulder.

Oh shit.

With nothing to lose, he spun around to throw a desperate punch at Sharday or Isadora, but instead found himself face-to-face with Phoenix Aurora.

He gasped in relief on finding the housekeeper here in the kitchen, because in his haste to escape from the house, he'd forgotten all about her.

Thankfully, considering the current situation, this time the woman had her clothes on.

"We need to get out of here!" he told her desperately. "There's intruders in the house."

"Intruders?" she asked. "Where?"

"They're downstairs in the basement." Billy turned back to the kitchen door. "But, something's wrong with this door! I dunno what the matter is, but—"

"The door won't let you out," Phoenix filled in for him. "Yeah, I know. I sensed there were others in here, uninvited others."

Billy grabbed hold of her arm. "Come on, let's try one of the other exits. Those two bitches are armed and crazy!"

But the housekeeper wagged a finger at him. "That won't help. At the moment, there's no way out of this building. There's no need to be so nervous, baby. I'll take care of your two pursuers."

Phoenix Aurora spoke with such seeming unconcern about the crisis that Billy believed her.

"Come to me," she told him sweetly and with gesturing arms. "Come to momma, momma knows exactly what a young man like you needs in every situation."

He stepped towards her and she embraced him.

At first her touch was as sensual as it had been upstairs, but then Billy sensed that something was wrong.

"What's going on?" he gasped when he discovered that he'd become stuck to the housekeeper, his chest, his belly, and his thighs seemingly glued to hers.

And to his horror, Phoenix Aurora's body had now become insubstantial. Suddenly she was something composed of black liquid and he felt himself sinking into her fluid essence, passing through her surface like a corpse thrown into the ocean, until finally he was completely inside of her.

And then the horrible pain began. Billy Evans felt like he was being ground between the infernal gears of some massive cosmic machine.

Billy's agony became endless, so endless that he had no idea exactly when he died.

And then the front of Phoenix Aurora's liquid form erupted like a volcano, spewing Billy's stripped and bloody bones out into the kitchen. His bones left her body with such force that they shattered cups and glasses on the kitchen counter, dislodged cutlery, dented pots and pans, and even punched a hole through the oven door.

Once the deluge of bones had ended, the liquid thing once more became solid Phoenix Aurora.

The housekeeper smiled at Billy's scattered bones with satisfaction, and then she walked over to shut the kitchen door.

CHAPTER 24

Paul, Jennifer, Duke, & Katrina

Katrina's black Subaru pulled up to the house and everyone got out.

"Yeah, this *is* quite the strange-looking place," Duke said. "No wonder Marko's mom hates it."

Paul gave Duke a narrow look. "Man, don't you start too. Jennifer's already sanding my ears down with that crap."

Duke looked inquiringly at Jennifer.

She grinned and explained: "We've a bet running about the house. He owes me a holiday in Florida if the house really is haunted. If he's right that it isn't, he gets extra sex."

Duke laughed and slapped Paul on the back. "I'm just having fun with you. Where I'm concerned a house is just a house is just a house. Where ghosts are concerned, I'm like you: I don't believe in them until I meet them in person, and in the past thirty-odd years of my life, I ain't met any ghosts yet."

"Hey, what about paranormal shows on TV?" Jennifer asked. "Don't those count with you?"

"Nah," Katrina answered for Duke, while twirling the ends of her red hair around a finger. "He says they're all faked."

Paul nodded his agreement. "With the new special effects, the fake stuff looks even better than the real thing."

"Tell me about it," Duke said. "Ladies, it's just like with tits—no one's sure who's got the real ones anymore, 'cos the fake ones almost always look better." He gave Katrina's rump a playful squeeze. "Not like I'm complaining tho'."

"So," Jennifer persisted. "If you happened to run into a ghost—I mean, indisputably—what would your reaction be?"

Duke thought about that for a moment. "I dunno . . . I've never really thought 'bout it that deeply."

"He'd probably ask for its autograph," Paul said. Then he jerked his finger towards the house. "C'mon, guys, let's get the beers inside and do some serious drinking."

"Hey, I got a better idea," Jennifer said, glancing up at the sky, as, all laden with bags and bottles, they walked over to the house. "I like the moon tonight. Let's do our drinking out here on the front porch."

Paul looked up at the sky too. The moon was nice and large, not yet full, but getting there.

"Yeah, why not?" he agreed, then looked at Duke and his girlfriend. "What do you guys think?"

"You know I don't care where I drink my damn beer," Duke said, settling himself on the top porch step and lifting a six-pack out of a bag. "Katrina's the choosy one."

"I'm game if y'all are," Katrina said. She sat down beside Duke and accepted a beer can from him.

"Okay, I'll be right back," Paul said. "I'll just go drop the rest of these drinks in the fridge to keep them chilled."

"And I gotta use the little girls' room," Jennifer chirped up with a pressed look on her face.

"Tell Billy to join us out here," Duke said. "And when those friends of his arrive, we'll have us quite the drinking party tonight."

CHAPTER 25

Paul

Once Jennifer had hurried off to the bathroom, Paul walked through the house to the kitchen to drop off the bags.

How come I didn't notice that before? he wondered on seeing that the oven's glass window had a hole through it, sort of like the kind of holes that bullets left in car windshields, a circular puncture framed by a spiderweb of cracks. *Did one of Marko's goons do some shooting in here?*

In addition to this, he noticed several broken drinking glasses in the sink.

He shook his head.

I'm certain those weren't in there when we arrived. Oops, Billy had better not wreck Marko's house!

Paul put the beers away in the fridge and left the kitchen to go find Billy.

Where is the kid anyway? Upstairs, downstairs, or in . . .

Then Paul heard a soft tapping sound coming from behind the basement door, along with a voice that was softly cussing.

Oh, here he is! The kid's locked himself in!

Paul reached for the lock on the door, and without taking the time to consider *how* Billy could have locked himself down in the basement, he unlocked the door.

"Hey, Billy!"

But it wasn't Billy down there.

Paul stared in surprise at the two women who stepped out of the basement.

"Thanks for letting us out of there," the one with the gun told him.

"Yeah," the other woman agreed. "Sharday and I have been trying to figure out how to shoot the lock off without alerting the neighbors."

CHAPTER 26

Paul, Sharday, & Isadora

"Listen," Paul said, once he'd determined that the two women were intruders and not Billy's expected friends. "You two ladies don't wanna do this: this house belongs to Marko Velli. Whatever else you wanna do in your life, pissing my brother-in-law ain't one of 'em."

"Shut up, we don't give a fuck," the blond woman told him.

The two women were holding the gun on him and had warned him to keep his voice down, or else . . .

Paul wondered what the fuck was going on.

The one thing I don't need now is a shootout. I should've brought a gun along. But who the hell ever imagines that anyone, and I mean anyone, would be suicidal enough to break into one of Marko's homes?

But apparently these two women were. The black one named Sharday had just dispatched her battered-and-blonde friend named Isadora to go to see where Jennifer was.

Paul had refused to volunteer the info by himself. He'd said he didn't know.

Seeing as they'd been so concerned about alerting the neighbors, I don't see them shooting us, but you can never tell what a person with a gun might do. Guns make people feel like they're God Almighty, with the power of life and death over other mortals.

Isadora hurried back over to them. "I don't see his girlfriend out there, but there's two other people, a guy and a redhead."

"Shit!" Sharday spat. "This just keeps getting more and more complicated.

"Listen, ladies," Paul said as calmly as he could manage. "I don't know who you two are, and I don't wanna know. Can you please just leave? For your info, we're expecting a party of at least four more people here tonight. Possibly five or six. What are you gonna do— shoot everyone?"

"He's got a point," Isadora said. "We can't kill everyone who comes here."

"Ladies," Paul went on, trying to leverage on Isadora's display of common sense, "I already told you this house belongs to my brother-in-law Marko Velli. For your information, Marko Velli is the most ruthless gangster in the USA. What the hell do you gain by pissing him off? You gain nothing except a concrete dress and a watery grave. Trust me, I've seen it—"

"Shut up!" Sharday told him, sticking the gun in Paul's throat.

Paul shut up.

"You know, I think he's right," Isadora told her. "We've already accomplished what we came here for. Let's just leave."

"We *can't* just leave. We need to find Billy and scare some sense into him. I made the mistake of telling him exactly who we are and what we've done. What if he decides to snitch on us to the cops?"

"Billy won't say a thing," Paul dared say. "Listen—"

"Shut the fuck up! I won't warn you again!" Sharday said, jamming the gun hard into Paul's throat. "Listen," she told him, "what we're gonna do now is, you're gonna follow us to the front door and convince your two friends out there to come inside the house." She pulled the gun away from Paul's throat, and waved it at him. "Get moving. And no tricks, or else . . ."

Paul nodded and let them steer him to the door.

He walked in front, with Isadora on his left, while Sharday walked behind him, with the gun poking into his back. Paul was relieved that the duo were now distracted from looking for Jennifer.

Hopefully, she'll come out of the bathroom, see what's going on, and phone Marko to send help. I hate the thought of what's gonna happen to these two ladies once Marko discovers they broke into his house, but I guess it can't be helped now.

They reached the front door and Sharday groaned.

"Shit, Dora, I thought you said there were just two people out there, where did the third person come from?"

"Oh, that's just his girlfriend," Isadora said. "She must've stepped out of view for a moment when I checked earlier."

"Duh. His girlfriend is a *blonde* like you. This woman has black hair."

"Really? Well then, who is she?"

Sharday and Isadora turned to look at Paul.

Paul shrugged. "She's our housekeeper. I'd forgotten she was here."

Out on the front porch, Phoenix Aurora was engaging Duke and Katrina in conversation. All three of them were laughing at something Katrina had said.

And then, all of a sudden, Phoenix Aurora expanded like she was a balloon, a balloon with long tentacles.

CHAPTER 27

Duke

The transformation from pretty woman to revolting monstrosity occurred so fast that for several seconds afterward Duke imagined he was watching a 3-D movie at the downtown multiplex. Then that perspective shifted slightly, to the feeling that he and Katrina were actually starring in said movie.

And then, with the bubble of his incomprehension still very much intact, Duke Higgins realized that this nightmare was real life.

But still, he couldn't overlook the movie comparison. The woman—she'd said she was the housekeeper here—had shapeshifted into the horror that now faced them with the ease of CGI special FX, with the sole difference being that Duke had no need to suspend disbelief.

This shit is for real!

He found it difficult to comprehend the thing. In a way, it was still the housekeeper—it had something of her particular feminine essence about it. And yet, this bloated monstrosity with waving tentacles and a dripping maw in its middle—he honestly couldn't call the opening a mouth—was clearly otherworldly.

It had no head, except if its entire body was its head. Above the maw were two huge eyes with—horror of horrors—long feminine eyelashes. Clearly the housekeeper's own eyes, as Duke recalled them, but twenty times larger.

The thing was about Duke's height, with most of its bulk being its width, and then of course there were its tentacles, which were innumerable and of different sizes. Some of the monster's tentacles were extensions of its body surface, while others protruded from its mouth, like black tongues. It balanced on several fat tentacles like they were feet.

A demon! Duke thought to himself. *It's a demon! That damn woman was a demon!*

"The house welcomes you both," the monster was saying, speaking clearly in the housekeeper's pleasant voice. "But once you arrive here; you must stay. Hardly anyone one ever leaves here."

The words made little sense to Duke.

But if I know one thing, he thought, *I know it's time to get the fuck out of here!*

Beside him, Katrina was trembling and whimpering. Though more than capable of looking after herself in everyday matters, she wasn't any sort of a movie 'final girl,' that heroine who kicked the shit out the monster that had butchered everyone else in the horror movie.

Duke and Katrina had both leapt up in alarm on the housekeeper's transformation.

Duke reached out an arm and tapped Katrina's shoulder.

"Listen, babe," he whispered. "We're gonna run for the car now. Gimme your car keys."

"They're still in the igni—"

The monster struck then. It lashed out at them with fat black tentacles coming from both left and right.

The tentacle aimed at Katrina instantly snared her, but Duke was more fortunate. While attempting to evade capture, he tripped over the edge of the porch and fell backward into the flowerbed beside it. The tentacle that had missed Duke swished through the air and doubled the monster's hold on Katrina instead.

Duke was back on his feet almost immediately, regretting that he'd left his gun back at the motel.

Also, his brush with the monster's tentacles had revealed that they had concealed hooks.

If they get hold of me, it'll be a hell of a job getting free of 'em.

Meanwhile, the monster had Katrina up in the air, her sandals two feet off of the ground. She screamed in terror, and it slapped her face with a tentacle, which tore her skin open and made her scream even louder.

Duke ran back around the front porch to its steps, wondering how to intervene before the creature hurt his girlfriend.

But then, before Duke could figure out any kind of offensive tactic that wouldn't prove suicidal to he and Katrina, the impossible thing on the front porch ripped Katrina's left leg right off of her body.

The monster kept its grip on Katrina, but flung the severed leg away.

With her leg gone, Katrina began yelling loudly enough now to wake the entirety of Raynham and the southern city of Taunton also.

Duke looked over at the front door. There was no one behind it.

Duke didn't get it:

At the very least, the noise should've alerted Paul and Jenny and Billy that something's amiss. But the house and the neighborhood seem as quiet as if all the noise is being restricted to this front porch area.

All of this was happening in a rush, but to Duke it had the quality of a slow dream, in which every detail possesses an absurd crystal clarity.

"No one leaves here," the monster said in a satisfied voice, while blood squirted from Katrina's left hip joint.

"Duke, help!" she gasped in a voice that sounded like she was already halfway through death's door.

Katrina's severed leg had dropped near Duke, and, desperate to save her using any means possible, Duke decided to use her leg as a weapon against the creature.

It should make a good club at least!

But as he bent to pick up the leg, the monster locked a tentacle around Katrina's forehead. Katrina's scream of additional anguish made Duke stop what he was doing and watch her torment instead.

Blood was leaking from the deep piercings that the tentacle's hooks had made in her head. And now the black tentacle was pulling her head up, up, inexorably up.

Duke watched it happen. While Katrina's eyes bugged out in total terror, her neck extended like a rubber band, but one that had no recoil. He heard the sound of her neck vertebrae popping while her flesh stretched like taffy, and then in a gush of blood, her neck reached the point of no return and snapped in two and her head popped free of her body.

"Oh no, Katrina!" Duke moaned.

"Nobody leaves here," the monster said and flung the severed head at Duke.

Duke wasn't expecting this latter action. The head and neck came whirling at him and smacked him square in the face. The impact knocked Duke head over heels, backwards and down the porch steps and left him sprawling on the parking lot gravel.

Duke lay there stunned. And the monster moved closer to him, flowing down the porch steps like spilled oil.

CHAPTER 28

Paul, Jennifer, Isadora, & Sharday

Inside the house, the three people watching through the glass portion of the front door were all struck speechless by what they were witnessing.

And witness the horror was all they could do. The front door was now sealed shut. No matter how much Paul turned the key in the lock and heard it click open, the door itself remained immobile in its frame as if it was welded shut.

So, they stood gaping, each of them thinking they were slowly going mad.

"What the fuck is that thing?" someone said finally. It could've been any one of them speaking, and the person who asked the question didn't even realize afterward that they'd spoken.

Paul, Sharday, and Isadora watched the black monstrosity drop Katrina's headless body on the front porch and flow down the porch steps towards Duke.

For a few moments it looked like Duke was a goner also. But Duke was tough and resourceful. He played possum and let the monster think he was dead, and then right at the moment when the thing struck at him, he leapt up and ran.

The creature seemed to overbalance, and its attempt to right itself gave Duke Higgins sufficient time to run to the black Subaru and drive off.

"Can someone please explain what's going on?" Paul said finally.

"That's supposed to be our line," Isadora whispered in shock. "This is *your* place; we met you here."

"And you just said she's *your* housekeeper," Sharday added.

Neither Sharday nor Isadora's reply was spoken in anger. Sharday had lowered her revolver away from Paul the moment the housekeeper had become a monster.

Isadora now tapped Sharday meaningfully on the shoulder. "Remember when earlier I said that this house seemed to want us to enter it?" she asked.

"I do. I should've listened to you then."

The monster was still outside, but while they watched, it once more became Phoenix Aurora. The housekeeper stared out at the road like she could see Duke's departing black car through the intervening houses and trees.

"Hey, did you ladies notice anything weird just now?" Paul asked.

Sharday scowled at him. "Other than that thing out there tearing that poor woman apart?"

Paul shook his head. "No. I mean that all the while that she—it, whatever—was killing Katrina out there, we didn't hear the sound of it inside here. Not a damn peep."

"Yeah, that's right," Sharday agreed with a puzzled look on her face. "I didn't even hear the sound of her boyfriend driving off just now. How is that possible?"

Jennifer returned from the bathroom then.

"Hey, guys, what's happening here?"

Paul quickly got between her and the door. He suspected that she'd likely faint if she got a look at Katrina's corpse.

Katrina smiled at Sharday and Isadora. "Oh, you guys must be Aaron's party."

Sharday rolled her eyes. "Everyone we meet here keeps saying that. We're not with Aaron; we're uninvited guests."

"And as to what's going on, babe," Paul said softly, "we've got a very serious problem. A massive problem."

But Jennifer didn't hear what he said. She was staring wide-eyed at Isadora, who was staring wide-eyed back at her.

Then they leapt forward and hugged each other tight.

"Dora, what the hell are *you* doing here?" Jennifer asked after they'd separated.

"Jenny, it really is you?" What are *you* doing here?"

The two women held each other at arm's length with happiness on their faces.

"So, you two know each other?" Sharday asked suspiciously, as if she suspected the pair were old lovers.

"Yeah, we once worked together at Westall Shipping," Isadora told her.

"The plot thickens like molasses," Paul said.

Jennifer was meanwhile, examining Isadora's battered face. "Who the hell beat you up like this? Are you still with deadbeat Joe?"

Isadora shook her head. "Not any more, thank God. Joe recently died in a fatal accident."

"It couldn't've happened to a nicer person," Jennifer said in mock seriousness.

Suspecting that if he didn't step in, their blissful reminiscence might go on forever, Paul tapped Jennifer forcefully on the shoulder.

"What?" she asked without looking at him.

"Darling, we have a problem," he told her patiently.

Jennifer now paid him some attention. "What's the matter?"

"Best if you see for yourself," Paul told her, stepping aside so that she could peek out through the door's glass window.

Jennifer looked that way and her jaw immediately dropped.

"What the . . .?" she gasped and looked horrified.

Paul, who'd intended to update Jennifer's state of mind by showing her Katrina's remains lying on the ground outside, himself turned around to look out through the door and was instantly as shocked as she was.

And she hasn't even seen Katrina out there yet!

With her body blocking off the front porch from view, Phoenix Aurora was walking in through the solid door of the house as if it didn't exist.

"Wha-wha-wha?" Jennifer said, backing away from the others.

Paul made sure to keep an eye on her. "Like I said, babe, we have a problem."

Once fully through the front door, the housekeeper smiled at them all.

"Who are you really?" Paul asked her.

"What are you?" Sharday added.

"Why . . . why . . .?" Isadora sputtered.

"I'll keep this short and to the point," Phoenix Aurora told them: "This house has claimed you all for its own."

"Some additional info would be nice here," Isadora said, while inching backwards like Jennifer was doing.

Phoenix Aurora nodded at her, and said: "This house is alive. It is a living entity, a literal house from hell in the human world. It needs a regular diet of human flesh and blood and pain to survive here. And I, the housekeeper, provide it with that human essence on a regular basis. And in this particular cycle, the flesh and blood and agony it will have for sustenance is yours." She laughed and added, "There is no

116

escape from the house tonight for any of you. Tonight, you will all die here."

"Like hell I will," Sharday said angrily. And before any of the others could intervene and stop her, she'd raised her gun and shot the housekeeper in the face.

CHAPTER 29

Paul, Jennifer, Isadora, & Sharday cont'd . . .

Well, it was as good an escape plan as any, Paul told himself after Sharday had put two bullets in Phoenix Aurora's head. *Not like it's made much difference. Not like I expected shooting the bitch would make ANY difference; not after what she did to Katrina.*

The gunshots had caused Phoenix Aurora to lose her balance and to stagger backward, but she was still standing and very far from dead.

However, Phoenix had two bullet holes in her forehead and there was now a black mess painting the wall beside her, caused by the slugs' exit from the rear of her head, which suggested to Paul that Phoenix must also have massive exit wounds back there, though he was on the wrong side of her to confirm this visually.

The black sludge that had exited her head and painted the wall also didn't look like any brains that Paul had ever seen before.

Phoenix frowned at Sharday. Sharday kept her gun pointed at her.

Paul waved at Sharday. "Put the gun down; we clearly can't kill her with it. You just tried and failed."

Sharday looked undecided. "I'm not about dying here like she just said." She looked defiantly at Paul and Jennifer. "Maybe you two don't mind, but I ain't gonna be this bitch's bitch."

Now, Phoenix Aurora smiled at Sharday.

"Oh, come on, don't be like that," she said in a honeyed voice. "I, for one, totally abhor girl-on-girl violence."

"So, what do you call what you did to that poor woman outside just now?" Sharday asked, her dusky face torn between fear, worry, and anger. "True romance?"

"Sometimes the beast within gets the better of me and I have to let it out," Phoenix said, stepping close to Sharday and pushing her gun arm down. "But I'm not always like that. Just like you, I like girls. I like to talk to them, I like to know them intimately, and . . ." she leaned in close to Sharday and whispered loudly . . . "and, best of all, I like to fuck them."

While this insane interaction was occurring—insane because half of the rear of the housekeeper's head was missing and there was black goo dribbling from both the massive hole at the back of her skull and the two bullet holes in her forehead—Jennifer dashed over to Paul' side.

"What woman outside is she talking about?" she whispered to him. "Did she do something nasty to Katrina?"

In response, Paul tapped the front door and indicated with a hand gesture that she look outside.

Jennifer peered through the glass and gasped loudly. Then she began sobbing like a baby.

Paul at first moved to comfort her, but then he stopped. The housekeeper's weird interaction with Sharday entranced him. He felt somewhat hypnotized by her voice and he suspected that Sharday did too.

"I have a girlfriend," Sharday said in a confused voice, while Phoenix Aurora gently stroked her cheek. "I love Isadora."

"That's fine," Phoenix said. "Isadora can either watch us, or she can join in."

Sharday looked into Phoenix's eyes and apparently liked what she saw there. "What did you mean, we belong to the house now?" she asked in a childlike voice. We just wanna go home."

"Don't worry about it," Phoenix Aurora told her. "Let's be lovers, okay?"

"Okay," Sharday agreed, and just like that, she and Phoenix Aurora were suddenly kissing, while Paul felt a thousand and one alarm bells ringing in his head and had the realization that Phoenix Aurora had just sucker-punched the black woman in the worst way possible.

Paul felt nothing erotic about the lesbian scene before him, nothing except the deep apprehension of bad things to come. He stepped close to Jennifer and took her in his arms, scared at what was going to result from Phoenix Aurora's kissing Sharday.

Sharday herself now understood that she'd been fooled. All of a sudden, her eyes widened in shock and she pulled her lips off of Phoenix Aurora's lips.

"What have you done to me, you bitch?" Sharday gasped.

Phoenix Aurora laughed. "I've just given you a priceless gift, darling. The gift of death."

Sharday began raising her gun to shoot the housekeeper, but before her arm straightened out, she was seized by weird tremors. The tremors racked her body from head to foot.

As Sharday stood there vibrating like a bell, large bulges began to appear across her body. First one part of her head or breasts or belly or arm or leg would bulge out to the height of about six inches or so, and then the bulge would sink back down and somewhere else would bulge out instead. The bulging clearly hurt because Sharday was howling in pain.

With tears in her eyes, Isadora ran over to Phoenix Aurora and grabbed her arm. "Stop it, stop torturing her! Stop right now!" she pleaded.

Phoenix brushed her off effortlessly. "Don't worry, her torment is almost over," she replied.

Almost immediately after she said this, Sharday Brooks wailed like an air-raid siren and then she exploded.

Bits of Sharday flew everywhere and splattered everyone present there, Phoenix Aurora inclusive.

Isadora immediately fainted and collapsed on the floor.

Paul stood there, wiping chunks of Sharday Brooks from off of he and Jennifer's faces and clothes.

He looked around at the crazy scene that had resulted from Sharday's death.

Sharday's scattered remains were now embedded in the walls of the house. Looking up, Paul saw her skull stuck in the ceiling, dripping blood down into the foyer. Half of her ribcage jutted out of the wall on his left, while her intestines had flown across the living room and were draped over the rear of a couch.

Both of Sharday's feet were still in her boots. One boot/foot was right-side-up but sunk deep into the floor as if hammered there, so that now its ripped top was level with the rug. Her other foot/boot was overturned on the opposite side of the entrance hall, with its toes deeply embedded in a hung painting of the Massachusetts countryside. This latter boot's/foot's similarity to a leaky faucet was emphasized by the blood dripping from it onto a small table beside the wall.

Strangest, craziest of all, to Paul's mind, was the fact that Sharday's right hand was stuck into the wall down the hallway, and it still gripped her revolver.

He and the others were standing in her blood.

So, Marko wanted to know if his house is haunted or not. I think we can tell him a definite yes!

"Oh my God, Paul, what are we gonna do?" Jennifer asked, tugging on his arm.

"We need to find a way out of here," Paul told her.

It now occurred to him that the reason why none of them had attempted to flee since realizing that the housekeeper was a monster in human form, was because either she, or this 'Hell House' was exerting some subtle mind control on them all. (Paul now recalled the weird way that the woman had twice personalized the building during their first conversations.)

"Did you need to do that?" he asked Phoenix Aurora, while gesturing around at the mess that two minutes ago had been a human being like himself. "Did you honestly have to?"

"She damaged me a little," came the disinterested reply. "I needed to repair myself and I have." She gestured at her head, and Paul saw that the damage was indeed gone. No nasty black-jelly-full holes wherever anymore.

"And as for the rest of you," the hellish housekeeper said. "Let me explain how this—"

Distracted by something, she turned around without completing her statement.

Then, speaking over her shoulder, she told them: "Oh, good, your other friends have arrived too."

Paul looked out through the door and saw two vehicles turning into the driveway. A blue sedan in front and a white pickup truck behind it. There was still no sound, just the visual.

Paul stared back at Sharday's remains and wondered how much worse things would get tonight.

We need to find a way out of here. And soonest. Before what happened to her, happens to the rest of us. And . . . (an absence that their problems had so far made insignificant) Where *the hell is Billy?*

"Now the real fun begins," Phoenix Aurora said.

Paul cringed on seeing the delighted smile on her face.

CHAPTER 30

Duke

The Sunflower Motel, Duke Higgins's accommodation for the night, was located at the far end of Carver Street, the same street that Marko's 'Hell House' was located on.

Duke drove there in an almost-blind panic, just maintaining enough self-control over himself to not skid off the road and wrap Katrina's Subaru around a tree.

No, that didn't . . . what the hell was that!? Oh, my God no . . . Shit, Katrina! It got my baby Katrina!

The time was now getting to about 9 p.m. and the motel parking lot had several cars driving in and out of it.

At the entrance to the motel, Duke had to wait for a few seconds as a long white van rolled out of the motel driveway into the road. The van's driver—an old, old man who looked to be like a hundred years old, but whose blue eyes projected a disturbing vitality—gave Duke an odd look, and then honked his horn at him.

The horn sound made Duke jerk up like he'd seen a ghost. The moment was made creepier by the fact that the nearby streetlight made the old driver look almost ethereal, like he'd exited his grave to come drive his van.

It slowly filtered through Duke's mind that the old man was staring oddly at him because he had some of Katrina's blood on his face and his clothes.

Oh Katrina! Oh . . . Katrina!

Duke gripped his steering wheel with rigid hands and somehow got the car safely parked in front of his motel room. Then he opened the door, hurried inside and put the chain on the door.

CHAPTER 31

The Arrivers

"I still can't get Billy on the phone," Aaron informed the others after one more try.

"Doesn't matter; we're here now," Bobbi told him. She checked the time on her watch and added, "Not too early and not too late."

They all got out of the car and looked at the house. A short while later, Rosa Perez and Cedric Hayes joined them.

"Cool joint," Cedric said.

"Yeah," Rosa agreed. "It gives me a weird vibe tho'."

"Please, don't you start with that too," Erica told Rosa.

"What do you mean?" Rosa asked.

"All the way over here," Erica replied, "Tom's been trying to terrify us with tales about this place, which we can now all see, is just a regular house."

Aaron studied the house in some detail. "You know, I think if it looks creepy, it's just 'cos it's nighttime."

"You're right," Cedric agreed, processing the view with a photographer's expert eye. "You got all of these trees and the moon too, and it creates a weird lighting effect."

"Whatever you say, dude," Tom said. "Guys, let's get our stuff unpacked and check into the Hell Hotel."

"Tom," Bobbi said while grasping her pendant as if for protection from evil, "if you don't stop trying to frighten me, I'll murder you before the witch and the ghosts do."

Everyone laughed and Rosa said: " 'The Witch and the Ghosts.' That'd make a great title for a book or a movie."

CHAPTER 32

The Loud Silence

Screw this! Paul decided when he saw the six young people who'd gotten down from the vehicles. *I'm not just leaving those kids to die.*

He began yelling to attract the attention of the six new arrivals: "HEY, OUT THERE! BACK UP AND DRIVE OFF! DON'T COME IN HERE! DON'T COME IN THE HOUSE!!"

After a few seconds, Jennifer caught on to what he was doing and joined in. As did Isadora, who'd now revived from her faint and kept watching the housekeeper with undisguised hatred.

Isadora made no attempt to attack the housekeeper though. Sharday's brutally dispersed remains were too potent a deterrent and a reminder of what might happen to her too if she angered the demon-woman.

"LISTEN, GO AWAY! GO AWAY!" Isadora yelled with all the force of her lungs. "DON'T COME IN THIS PLACE OR YOU'LL NEVER GET OUT!!"

While they all thus screamed, Phoenix Aurora laughed and laughed.

Paul finally gave up trying to attract the attention of the new arrivals, who were now unloading their luggage from their vehicles. He'd almost yelled himself hoarse and yet the six youths outside the house showed no sign of hearing a thing.

After a while Jennifer and Isadora both quit yelling too.

"Why can't they hear us?" Isadora angrily asked the housekeeper.

Phoenix Aurora smiled coolly at them all. "To this house, screams of pain and terror are sweet music and so it absorbs them all."

"I wish your damn house would absorb *you*," Isadora said with venom.

Paul was trying to figure out what next to try, when he felt Jennifer tugging on his sleeve.

"Don't worry about it," she whispered to him. "She's not that smart."

"What do you mean?" he whispered back.

"They'll see Katrina's corpse on the front porch," Jennifer whispered. "It's impossible to miss."

Paul felt relieved. "Yes, a headless corpse is a heads-up if ever there was one," he agreed. "Once they see it, this place will be swarming with cops in minutes."

But then, he saw that Phoenix Aurora was smiling at Jennifer.

"I completely forgot about that," the housekeeper told Jennifer. "Thanks for reminding me—I'll just clean up my mess now. I am the housekeeper for this building after all. Keeping the yard tidy is part of what I do." She laughed. "I'm not always so absentminded; that's why you didn't find Billy's corpse in the kitchen. It's just that there's just a lot of people to keep track of tonight."

Paul felt the fight drain out of him.

She's killed Billy too? What the hell are we gonna do to stop her?

Isadora's frustration was so great that she now turned away from everyone and began kicking the wall.

Phoenix Aurora waved a hand at the front porch.

And just like that, the three pieces of Katrina's body and her spilled blood started to fade from view.

Paul paid closer attention to what was going on. He soon realized that Katrina's corpse wasn't actually fading away, but was rather being absorbed into the stone flooring of the porch. Her skin, her flesh and her clothing were losing their natural colors and turning grey as rock, before finally seeming to liquify and flatten against the stonework and become one with it.

Fuck! Paul thought.

CHAPTER 33

Cleanup

None of Aaron's party had yet noticed Katrina's gruesome remains. And so, none of them realized that the gory mess on the front porch had become part of the building they were about entering into.

CHAPTER 34

Captives . . .

"Well, I guess I'd better go welcome my new guests," Phoenix Aurora told her three surviving captives. And then she walked out through the shut door again.

"I've felt helpless many times before," Jennifer said as they watched the demonic housekeeper descend the porch steps and head for the two vehicles. "But this must be the first time in my life that I feel so helpless that I could kill myself from frustration."

Paul nodded. "Yeah, honey, I feel the same way too. But there's gotta be something we can do to halt this insanity."

Jennifer pointed across at Isadora, who'd now stopped kicking the wall, but still stood facing it, motionless as a statue and with her hands bunched into fists by her sides.

Jennifer gave Paul an inquiring look and after he nodded back at her, she walked over to Isadora and gently turned her around.

Just like Isadora's shoes were red from stepping in Sharday's spilled blood, her eyes too were red from weeping. Jennifer hugged her tightly.

"I feel your pain," she told Isadora. "Her killing her like that was so unnecessary."

"She's simply a sadistic monster," Isadora moaned. "I mean she killed your friend Billy too. For no reason at all."

"I doubt it was for no reason," Paul disagreed angrily. "I suspect she fed him to this house, like she intends to do to the rest of us."

CHAPTER 35

Welcome . . .

Aaron noticed the woman the moment she stepped out through the front door of the house.

Stepped through it?

For a split-second Aaron's mind was a blank, then he did a doubletake, studying the woman as she descended the porch steps.

I'd have sworn that she didn't open the front door, but walked through it. But I haven't smoked any weed today, so that's impossible.

And so, Aaron shelved his crazy thoughts and didn't mention them to anyone else.

He studied her as she approached. Her back was to the porch lights, but diffuse illumination from the sides of the house revealed that she was very pretty. She was also tall and slender and graceful.

But, why does she also seem a little creepy? Dammit, all that silly ghost talk on the drive over is getting to me!

The woman was very close to them now and the others had also noticed her and ceased unloading their stuff from the two vehicles. Everyone gathered near Aaron.

"Hello, everyone!" she said when she reached them. "My name is Phoenix Aurora. I'm the housekeeper for this place and you're welcome here."

Her voice was gentle and warm and Aaron instantly felt himself drawn to her.

He shook her extended hand. Her fingers and palm felt soft and warm and . . . creepy?

"I'm Aaron and these are . . ." He gave everyone's names.

" 'Hey there!' 'Hi!' 'Hello!' " everyone greeted one after the other.

"Glad you could make it here today," Phoenix said. "Paul and Jennifer and Billy will be so delighted to see you all."

"Where is everyone?" Tom asked. "We've been trying to get Billy on the phone almost since we left Springfield, but his phone just goes to voicemail."

"Billy broke his phone," Phoenix Aurora said. "He was standing up on the rear balcony and dropped it over the balcony railing. The screen is fritzed."

"But no one else seems to be here at the house," Rosa pointed out. "I'd have expected them to come out to welcome us."

Aaron welcomed this observation. He'd been having similar thoughts.

Yep, girl, they do teach you guys the right stuff at the police academy.

The housekeeper shrugged. "Oh, they all stepped out for a walk." She gestured out at the street and then pointed left. "There's a McDonald's at the corner. Jennifer wanted a burger."

"Yeah, we passed it on our drive in," Cedric acknowledged. "So, they're all over there?"

"Either there or at the shopping center that's farther down Broadway Road."

Bobbi gave an exaggerated yawn. "I could do with a burger myself. It feels like forever ago since I last had a bite."

Aaron grinned at her and asked the housekeeper: "So, you're gonna let us into the house then?"

Phoenix Aurora nodded. "Of course. That's my job." But then she stopped speaking and stared at Bobbi, or more accurately, Aaron realized that she was staring at Bobbi's creepy necklace.

Then the housekeeper touched the weird pendant.

No one was prepared for what happened next. Without warning, the black octopus-like pendant began glowing with a vivid 'darklight.' The color it produced was otherworldly, like neon purple but much darker, as if shadows could be projected as light.

The necklace pulsed like a strobe. On off, on off, on off; with each flash lasting for about a second's duration, and with a similar period of dimness between its flashes.

Aaron gaped at the necklace's strange transformation, as did all the others.

Bobbi looked stunned. The intermittent flashes of light down on her chest gave her face a ghostly look.

"Does it use batteries?" she asked Phoenix Aurora. "The woman who sold it to me told me it has a strange power, but she had no idea what that power was or how to unlock it."

The housekeeper laughed. "No, it doesn't use batteries, it doesn't need any."

Everyone looked confused.

"So, how does it light up then without a power supply of some kind?" Tom asked.

Tom's question exactly mirrored what was in Aaron's mind.

That little pendant is giving out a lot of light with each pulse. For her to say that it isn't battery-powered is crazy.

"The necklace is simply reacting to the house," Phoenix Aurora explained. "It used to belong to Erin De Mornay, a woman who once owned this place." She smiled at Bobbi, her alluring face now made grotesque by the strobe effect. "I daresay your necklace recognizes the fact that it's come home again."

"But that's crazy," Erica said. "It's just a necklace."

"Of course it is," Phoenix Aurora agreed. "But remember, some inanimate objects are sensitive to their location. This is one of such objects. The pendant is resonating with the house. Sort of like a child that's just come home to mama and is beaming with delight."

As if it had worn itself out for the time being, the pulses from the black pendant were now reducing in both intensity and duration. Slowly the pendant returned to its previous inert state.

"So, it's true that Erin De Mornay was a witch?" Aaron asked the housekeeper.

The woman nodded. "Yes, she was. A very powerful witch indeed. One of the greatest of all time. Definitely not someone to mess with, even as a joke."

"So, what does my necklace do?" Bobbi asked in an awestruck voice, while rubbing her fingers across the pendant. "Do you know? I've been trying to activate it for months now, but with no success at all."

Phoenix Aurora nodded. "Yes, I do know what it does. And I'll tell you all after I get you settled inside the house." She laughed. "You all don't want my bosses to return and think I've been slacking in my duties, do you?"

Everyone laughed and went back to unloading the vehicles.

CHAPTER 36

Duke

Over at the Sunflower Motel, Duke Higgins paced his motel room while horrified thoughts paced through his mind. The thoughts jostled each other for prominence, bumping and cascading against the walls of Duke's sanity.

He kept seeing that black tentacled monster stretching out Katrina's neck like it was a length of rubber, kept hearing the horrible sounds of Katrina's neck vertebrae popping apart from each other and the nasty croak as Katrina died.

He kept seeing Katrina's blood spurting everywhere.

Duke Higgins tried to force the recollections from his mind, but they persecuted him in a relentless barrage of pictural carnage.

"What . . . what . . . what the hell do I do now? Yeah, my gun!"

He ran over and got his Glock out of his traveling bag. Holding the gun gave him some confidence. He was no longer unarmed, no longer prey to be preyed on.

He settled down and attempted to think better.

Bit by bit, Duke Higgins calmed himself down.

Hell no, I ain't survived the Boston gangland all these years by being cowardly, by running away from a fight, and I got the scars to prove it. This is just one more battle that I gotta fight.

The problem here was that Duke still didn't believe his own experience. Despite the fact that Duke Higgins had just fled the scene in Katrina's car, and that he knew her body was lying in at least three pieces back at Marko Velli's cursed house, in this rational universe that everyone lived in, it still made more sense to Duke to believe that he'd just had a vivid hallucination, and to expect Katrina Sanderson to knock on the motel room door bitching about how he'd freaked out and left her back at Marko's house when she'd just gone to use the bathroom.

What the hell is in that house that Marko bought? Duke wondered. And then, when he couldn't answer that one: *Okay, so what do I do now? Yeah, I better call the cops and report this—*

131

He'd already picked up his cellphone before he realized how dumb his distress call would sound:

"Hello, 9-1-1? I got a massive problem here. A giant black blob just tore my girlfriend's head off . . . "

What a fucking joke! The cops'll decide I did it. I'll be back on Cellblock 9 before I know it.

Instead, still half-gripped by a state of delusion, Duke called Katrina's phone.

Please, please answer the phone, baby! Please, please! he thought desperately as the phone rang and rang and rang and rang. *Please be okay! Please, let this just be a normal bad dream! Please let it be that none of that craziness happened back there!*

But Katrina's number didn't connect, but instead flipped over to her voice telling callers to leave her a message and she'd call them back when she got the chance.

Duke sat down on the motel room bed and brooded for a short while, then he got up and opened the fridge, looking for a drink.

The fridge was empty of liquor, which reminded Duke of the reason why he and Katrina had left the house in the first place tonight, which was to buy booze.

Cursing that fact, Duke opened the motel room door and walked out to the car, where he knew he had a bottle of J&B sitting in the back seat.

Duke retrieved this whiskey and returned to the motel room. After some consideration, he put the chain back on the door.

I'm going back to that house tonight, Duke told himself as he opened up the whiskey bottle. *In a short while, I'm walking back there, armed and very dangerous. Hallucination or demon, I'm gonna take out that monster that took out Katrina. An eye for an eye, a head for a head, and a tentacle for a leg.*

He looked around for a glass to pour the whiskey into, but then laughed at his stupidity and tilted the bottle to his lips.

Then he checked that his Glock was working right and clicked the safety off.

CHAPTER 37

Inside Hell House

Paul was currently having zero success with getting either Marko Velli or anyone else on the phone.

And this didn't apply to just Paul. Jennifer and Isadora were also trying desperately to phone out for help, but without any success either.

"We've no reception in here and I think we all know why that is," Jennifer said finally, then shook her head and put her cellphone back into her pants' pocket.

"Yeah, that's right," Paul agreed and put his cellphone away also.

They'd already tried the landline in the living room, but couldn't even get a dial tone.

Jennifer began walking around in a circle. Paul watched her for a while and then turned his attention back to what was happening outside the house.

"Dammit!" he heard Jennifer say all of a sudden.

Paul spun around to see what had annoyed her.

During her circular shuffle, Jennifer had moved too close to a denim-clad mass of dripping gore that jutted out of the wall.

To Paul's not-so-critical eye, the mess looked like maybe part of Sharday's liver and the jacket that had covered it.

"Dirty bitch," Jennifer said on realizing this too. "She could at least have cleaned up inside here also."

Paul shared her sentiments.

"She didn't clean up in here because she wants to continue to scare us," Isadora told them both. "She wants us frightened, terrified of both herself and of this house." Isadora gestured around at the exploded mess that used to be Sharday Brooks. "Ugh, I can't believe she did that to her. That was just so unnecessary and so mean."

Isadora seemed about to cry again, so Paul nodded to Jennifer, who went to her and hugged her to prevent a fresh outburst of tears.

Paul felt scared like he'd never been before in his life.

Okay, so (mostly because old habits die hard) he still didn't want to believe in ghosts, but what else could one make of this? He'd seen the housekeeper inflate like a balloon to kill Katrina and then explode Sharday like a grenade merely by kissing her.

How in the hell does that work? How are we gonna survive this? I gotta dial up a solution to our crisis and fast!

Confused for the moment as to what actions would take them all to safety, Paul looked out through the glass top half of the front door again. Phoenix Aurora was still holding a conversation with Billy's friends.

Earlier there'd been a weird interlude when a 'black kind of light' had begun flashing amidst the new arrivals, with the strange effect that each time it did so, Paul, Jennifer, and Isadora could see the skeletons inside the bodies of the people beside the cars. As if the 'black light' had x-ray qualities.

That had been incredibly creepy, but what was even more creepy was that, alone of the gathering, Phoenix Aurora had appeared to have no skeleton inside of her.

Paul felt a tap on his shoulder and turned back to face his companions. Isadora was the one who'd tapped him, and she had a hollow look in her eyes like someone had plugged her into the misery motherlode.

"Okay, so what are we gonna do now?" she asked him in a scared voice. "Just like Sharday said, I think it's dumb to wait here like rabbits expecting the big bad wolf to eat us."

"I agree with her," Jennifer told Paul, her own expression and voice only a few degrees less nervous than Isadora's. "What the hell do we do now?"

Before replying them, Paul looked past them both, at the walls of both the entrance hall that they stood in and part of the living room, where blood still dribbled down the walls from those parts of Sharday's corpse implanted in them.

The various organs stuck out from the walls like they were parts of a sculpture. The surreal effect filled Paul's mind with scary questions:

What kind of violent force can enable someone's kidney to penetrate a wall, even if it's a plasterboard wall? he wondered. *Or their lungs? It makes some sense if bones crack a wall—those are hard as nails—but an eyeball?* He grimaced at the sight of a brown eye peering at him from the wall on the right. *How does an eyeball crack a wall like it's as hard as a marble? How does a strip of soft muscle penetrate through the back of a chair?*

"Hey!" Isadora said, punching Paul on the arm to get his attention. Paul forced his focus back to their present troubles.

"What I think," he told the two women, "is that we three had better make tracks while that devil woman is otherwise occupied. Let's get the hell out of Dodge City while we've got a chance, and then try to warn Billy's friends to do the same."

"That's what I'm thinking too," Jennifer said. "But the reason why we're still standing here is because Phoenix tells us there's no way out of the house." She grabbed the front door handle and twisted it back and forth. "See? How do we escape from here if we're supernaturally locked in?"

"That's a great question," Isadora agreed. "Any ideas?" After she'd peeked through the door herself, she added, " 'Cos I dunno how much longer she's gonna be out there, and once she brings them in the house, we're all gonna be screwed together."

Paul winced at her choice of words, which painted the picture of their possible fates a little too well. "Let's try to prevent that orgy of blood and destruction, shall we?" he said.

"Guys, we really need to leave here before she comes back into the house," Isadora moaned pitifully. "I don't wanna end up like Sharday."

"I'd suggest that we check all the house exits, to see if they're really sealed off like Phoenix claims they are," Paul said in a urgent voice. "Okay, let's go."

Ridden like horses by that same sense of urgency, they moved off into the house.

Along the way, Paul stopped by Sharday's severed right hand, which still held her gun, although its wrist was implanted in the wall.

"Ugh, what are you doing?" Jennifer asked when he began prying the weapon from the fingers of the dead hand.

For her part, Isadora pointedly turned away from the sight of Paul manhandling her dead girlfriend's dead hand.

"Aside from the knives in the kitchen," Paul explained, "it's the main weapon we've got. I'm taking it with us."

"Be careful that it doesn't shoot you," Jennifer said and turned away also.

The brown corpse hand at first resisted letting the firearm go. Rather than this simply being a case of extreme rigor mortis, however, the hand's resistance to letting Paul have the gun seemed almost supernatural, and added layers to his worries and his fear. But he persisted and finally wrestled the weapon free of that viselike grip of dead female fingers and thumb.

Strips of clotting blood colored the revolver's grip, and even dangled from its bottom like tassels. This hardened blood had a revolting look and feel to it.

Paul wiped the blood off on his pants, and afterwards popped out the revolver's cylinder.

Two shots fired, four to go.

He slid the cylinder back into place and looked over at Isadora, who looked disgusted.

"Do you have any more bullets?" Paul asked her.

Isadora shook her head. "Not here—maybe outside in the car."

Paul slipped the gun into his pocket. "Okay, let's search. We're on the ground floor, so we'll search here first."

"The front door is out," Jennifer said, jerking her thumb over her shoulder. "We know that much."

"Which leaves the kitchen door and the back door," Paul said, and then he looked searchingly at Isadora and asked her, "You were down in the basement. Is there any additional exit down there?"

Isadora laughed coldly. "Not one that we'd wanna take out of here."

"What do you mean?" Jennifer asked her.

Isadora laughed some more. "I mean, that us trying to leave this house via the basement will be like jumping from the proverbial frying pan into the fire. I mean, the fires of hell."

Paul understood that she was telling them the truth and shivered.

It felt to him that by having this very necessary discussion they were wasting valuable time doing nothing, when in reality they were acting as fast as they could.

"Okay," he told Isadora. "I'll take your word for it that the basement is out. So now, we split up." He gestured left. "You two ladies check the kitchen door for an exit, and then, if that won't work, check the windows of the guest bedroom on this side of the house." He gestured the other way. "I'll check the back door and the other guest bedroom. I'll also see if there are any other exits on this ground floor."

"I'm really worried, baby," Jennifer told him. "What are we gonna do if none of the rooms we search have a way out of here?"

Paul pulled Jennifer close and hugged her and then kissed her hair. "Don't worry, honey," he said as soothingly as he could manage. "If we can't find a way out downstairs, we'll check upstairs too, and then, if that doesn't work out either, we'll try to break out through the walls or the ceiling or get up on the roof." He pushed Jennifer away from him. "Now, go! Go! Both of you!"

The two women ran off towards the kitchen.

After watching them for the briefest of moments, Paul hurried towards the back of the house to also search for a way out of this hellish place.

CHAPTER 38

Cleanup

Once Paul, Jennifer, and Isadora left the front room, the gory mess that had once been Sharday Brooks was absorbed into the building's walls, ceiling, and floor, as, unknown to the visitors outside, the housekeeper prepared the house for their arrival.

CHAPTER 39

Outside . . .

"Well, that's about everything we're taking out of the car," Aaron told Phoenix Aurora.

The housekeeper gave him a smile that made him a little weak at the knees.

Aaron had two bags of his own, as did Tom. Then there was the obligatory beer cooler, stocked up to the brim in case of emergencies, even though Billy had assured them that there would be more available to drink that they could handle.

However, Tom had *insisted* that the beer cooler make the trip with them. "Hunger we can handle, bro," he'd said, "but a lack of alcoholic beverages makes us dull boys."

Aaron had seconded that reasoning.

Other than those essential liquid purchases, the guys had several bags of potato chips and energy bars between them.

But the ladies . . .

In addition to their regular daily getup, Bobbi and Erica had brought along lots of clothes for their photo shoots.

Then they had their huge wheeled makeup case with them also.

"You're carrying this in for us," Erica had already told Aaron, indicating the makeup case. Then she'd giggled at his tormented expression and whispered in his ear. "Don't worry—Bobbi more than plans to make it up to you."

Those words had filled Aaron with more energy than he'd need to move twenty makeup cases into the house.

In the meantime, Phoenix Aurora was chatting to Tom about something. The pair stood a little apart from everyone and were talking in hushed sentences that were interspersed with lots of laugher and giggles.

Aaron tried to listen in on their conversation. He quit after he heard the phrases "Bermuda Triangle House," and "That's simply ridiculous hearsay."

Aaron felt a moment's return of the old worry, but then he stared at the house boldly. He shook the apprehension off.

It's just another house with a bad rep. A few druggies murder someone in there and next thing you know, everyone assumes it's the highway to hell. Do I really believe that? Well, I dunno, but thinking this way sure beats spending the entire weekend expecting to be sacrificed to the devil.

Logically satisfied for the moment, Aaron looked over at Cedric and Rosa. "I think we're all set. You guys ready too?"

Cedric nodded. "Ready to hit the house." A big muscular guy, Cedric had a large camera slung around his neck, had on a giant camping backpack, and was also gripping two large carryalls, along with a camera tripod.

Beside him, Rosa was carrying nothing, meaning that about half of the stuff that Cedric was carrying was hers. Girlfriend benefits, of course. Rosa seemed entranced with her cellphone.

Though Rosa was too preoccupied with whatever she was doing to see him, and Cedric was too preoccupied with Rosa to notice either, Aaron hid his amusement.

I wonder what sort of policewoman she'll make if she's this addicted to her cellphone. Maybe they'll put her on Facebook or Instagram patrol?

Aaron looked away from Rosa. Phoenix Aurora and Tom seemed have finished their whispered conversation.

"Alright, we're ready," Aaron told the housekeeper.

But Phoenix Aurora shook her head like she'd just remembered something.

"Is there a problem?" Erica asked her, with what Aaron decided was more than a hint of jealousy stemming from Tom's possible interest in the older woman.

"Nothing serious," the woman replied. "But you're gonna have to settle yourselves in the house."

"Is anything the matter?" Aaron asked also.

"Not at all," Phoenix replied with a gentle laugh. "Just some stuff that'd I'd forgotten about that I need to attend to for about half an hour." She gestured over at the house. "Please go in and make yourselves comfortable. There are two empty bedrooms upstairs and also two downstairs. Put your stuff in any of them that you like. In fact, I suggest the ladies all room upstairs; those bedrooms have the best bathrooms in the house."

"That's fine," Aaron said, though all of a sudden he felt a little weird again.

"And now you'll need to excuse me for a short while, while I handle that little mat—"

"Hey, I can't seem to get a phone signal," Rosa said out of the blue. "Can any of you guys?"

Erica, who had her phone in her hand, examined its screen. "No, I can't," she said after a moment. "That's odd. It was okay a short while ago."

"Guys, anyone else just lost their phone service?" Rosa asked.

Tom waved his phone at her. "No service here either. Verizon's gone AWOL."

"AT&T is AWOL too," Bobbi said after a while, then looked at Aaron. "You got a phone signal?"

He didn't bother getting his phone out. "I doubt it. Just like Tom, I'm also on Verizon."

Everyone turned to look at Cedric, who was the only person who'd not yet checked his cellphone. The black guy shook his head at them, and indicated the amount of stuff he was carrying. "Gimme a break, huh?"

Rosa fished in his pants pocket for his phone. His jeans were tight and his arms were in the way and so she had a lot of difficulty extracting the cellphone and kept twisting and turning her fingers in his pants to get a proper grip on it.

"Cedric has a boner, but no signal bars," she announced after succeeding.

"That's the result of you fiddling around down there," Cedric grunted in embarrassment. "I told y'all to gimme a break."

"Is this a normal thing here?" Bobbi asked Phoenix Aurora.

"What? Cedric getting boners once I touch him down there?" Rosa asked with an ingenuous smile on her lips. "I assure you that that's very normal."

"Babe, please," Cedric groaned.

"Oh, it happens sometimes," the housekeeper replied with a little smile. "There's an experimental government project around here that constantly interferes with cellphone reception. Rumor has it they're working on a beam that will knock UFOs out of the sky by disrupting their electrical signals."

"UFOs? You're joking right?" Aaron asked.

"But don't worry," Phoenix Aurora finished off. "All network service should be restored in thirty minutes or so."

Rosa groaned. "Thirty minutes? On the internet that's longer than eternity."

"I hope the reception remains off for quite a while," Cedric told her. "That way you can help me take care of the erection you just gave me while trying to get my phone out of my pocket. How a policewoman can mistake a cellphone for a penis is beyond me. You'll be crap on the Vice Squad."

Everyone laughed at that, with Erica pointing at Cedric in amusement, while he held a bag in front of his crotch.

And then, Tom asked, "Where'd she go?"

"Where did who go?" Erica asked.

"Phoenix Aurora."

Erica shrugged disinterestedly. "Well, she did say she had to go take care of some housekeeping stuff. So, she left. What about it?"

"Yeah, yeah," Tom agreed impatiently. "I heard her say she had stuff to do. But, guys, did any of you actually *see* her leave?"

Aaron looked from one of them to the next as they all looked around them.

From the looks on everyone's faces, it was crystal clear that nobody had seen Phoenix Aurora leave them.

"I don't care what anyone tells me," Erica said. "That woman wasn't a ghost." She stabbed Tom in the belly with her cellphone. "And you, stop ogling her and let's get into the house already. Just 'cos she's older don't mean that she's better than me at sucking . . ."

Then she got an 'Oops' look on her face and giggled: "TMI, guys. TMI, sorry."

Dragging Tom after her, Erica headed off towards the house.

After a few shrugs, Cedric and Rosa followed suit, as did Bobbi.

Aaron stood alone by the cars, bathed in moonlight, staring out at the street, trying to figure out how Phoenix Aurora had left them all here without anyone noticing her departure.

"Hey, Aaron, come on inside already," Bobbi said. "Are you planning on spending the night out here?"

He turned around. Bobbi was walking back toward him from the front porch. Behind her, the others had the front door open and were moving their stuff inside.

He accepted that he'd been so preoccupied with solving the puzzle of the housekeeper's leaving that he'd not noticed Bobbi's own approach.

Maybe that's the key to the puzzle?

Shaking his head, Aaron followed Bobbi to the house and dropped his bags beside hers on the front porch. Then, while Bobbi carried their things inside, Aaron walked back to the car to fetch the girls' wheeled makeup case.

And, wow, was the damn thing heavy.

CHAPTER 40

Duke . . . Reinterpreted

Duke woke up.

This wasn't one of those slow beer awakenings where you had to convince yourself to stop dreaming so you wouldn't piss your pants in bed.

No, this time, he was instantly awake and alert, like the intervening sleep had been imagination.

Also, Duke immediately felt like something was wrong.

Cold chills rippled up and down his spine. He sat up and checked the clock on the nightstand. 10 p.m. He looked over at the motel room door. It was locked and the chain was still on, exactly how he'd left it.

He looked through into the bathroom. That too looked normal.

So, what's the matter?

Then, Duke realized why he felt odd and facepalmed himself in disbelief.

I passed out for a few minutes. But, how could I?

Duke really didn't get how that was possible.

The last thing I remember, I was sitting on the edge of the bed drinking my J&B and now . . .

The bottle of whisky sat on the coffee table in the farther half of the room, with less than a quarter of its volume missing.

So how did I fall asleep like that? Exhaustion or what?

And then, Duke's perplexed frame of mind gave way to anger. He sat up in bed and looked around for his gun.

I gotta get back over there right away!

Duke spun around to a sudden rustling of the window drapes on his left, and that was when he realized that he wasn't alone in his motel room.

There was a naked woman in here with him, sitting in the chair to the right of the coffee table.

Duke did a doubletake and his confusion tripled.

Katrina? How in the world? What the . . .?

Finding Katrina here with him in their motel room after seeing her being murdered by a monster had a weird effect on Duke. He felt his mind stretching to its absolute limits, and then his thoughts compacted again.

Katrina is alive.

But no, she's not. Katrina is dead. This must be someone else.

Duke studied her for defects. He'd seen Katrina naked so many times that he instinctively knew every inch of her body.

But no, everything about her was right; each of her tattoos checked out correct.

Naked, Katrina was as breathtaking as ever. Her pale skin and red hair were simply perfect, and her face, lovely. And then of course she had such cute breasts, with their little brown nipples . . . the red pubic fur promising erotic delight.

Duke lost his doubts. He felt intense relief.

So, it really was just me seeing things, then?

But at the same time, a deep fear gripped Duke Higgins.

But if she came back alive, how the hell did she get in here? he wondered. Beside Katrina, the door was locked, the chain in place. *The window? But that's impossible!*

The window was guarded by a lattice; only the night breezes that were teasing the drapes to and fro could possibly have gotten in that way. So how? He looked up; there were no openings in the ceiling.

Katrina had gotten up and was walking towards him. Duke resisted the urge to get up from the bed and flee from her.

"Oh, baby, you've finally woken up," Katrina said. Her voice was soft and reassuring. "You seemed to be having the most horrible nightmare."

A nightmare? I was asleep? Duke ran his mind through that scenario. *I dreamed all of that? But how?*

There was, of course, a way to confirm this once and for all.

If I really was over at some Hell House a short while ago, my hands and clothes will have blood on 'em.

Duke examined his hands. His hands were spotless. There was just a little grease under his fingernails from when he'd been fiddling with the car engine that morning. Similarly, his clothes had no blood on them.

Seeing as the first two examinations checked out negative, he didn't bother going to look at his reflection in the bathroom mirror.

"I dreamt all of that?" he asked Katrina.

Katrina gave him a worried look. "All of what, baby?"

"I dream that you were . . . and a haunted house and . . ." Duke shut up and instead waved his hand at her. "Don't bother, sweetie; you don't wanna know."

She nodded. "Okay, if you say so. We were about going to the liquor store to get something to drink because you were out of whiskey and then somehow you fell asleep. I didn't wake you 'cos you've been driving all day."

Out of whiskey? But that bottle of J&B is almost full!

He looked behind her to confirm that fact.

But no, where Duke had previously noted that the whiskey bottle was over three-quarters filled, now it was nine-tenths empty.

Dammit. I really was dreaming! What a frigging doozie of a dream too. I coulda swore it all happened. Me and Kat meeting up with Paul and Jenny and going back to that house and . . .

Okay, so it all checked out.

With that settled, Duke tried to relax, but he still found it hard to do so, because worryingly, Katrina was holding a large knife in her right hand.

"What are you doing with the knife?" he asked Katrina.

She grinned, flashing pretty white teeth. "Nothing. I found it in the closet after you passed out." She flung the knife dismissively onto the bed. "There's an axe in there too. Maybe the last renter of this room was a serial killer."

Duke nodded. He felt sheepish now.

Katrina stepped up close to him and kissed him. "I dunno what's come over me, Duke, but I need you right now." She pulled his face to hers and kissed him wetly on the lips.

He felt her tongue forcing its way between his lips and immediately grabbed her ass and pulled her closer. Nine months behind bars, nine months without a woman, had left Duke as randy as a rabbit. Since they'd been driving around, Katrina had been complaining that he was constantly making her sore.

She brushed against him, her smell of femininity filling his nostrils. His manhood leapt to painful erection in his pants.

Katrina's beauty pinned him to the bed like a bug on a corkboard. He felt like he was sinking into her lust-filled expression—she had such big beautiful eyes.

But still . . .

Duke stared at the knife she'd dropped on the bed. He had a sudden premonition of danger. For a few seconds, something once more struck him as not being quite right in this scenario. He sensed the wrongness with clarity. It felt as if he'd woken up from the deepest layer of a nightmare only to slip into another, even deeper one.

During these fleeting seconds while he kissed Katrina, Duke felt that the smartest thing for him to do right now was to dash across the room and outside into the night.

And then put a thousand miles between himself and her and this motel room.

But lust won out; along with that sense of needing to be sensible. Running away from a nightmare had to be the dumbest thing in the world.

Katrina had been trying to slide Duke's pants off. Now, realizing his mind was elsewhere, she stopped and gave him a pissed-off look. "Hey, pay attention to me. You've been after me all week for some pussy and now that I'm horny, you can't concentrate."

"The knife worries me," he told her. "It looks so damned sharp. I don't want us cutting ourselves while we're having fun."

Katrina seemed like she might say something cutting to him in return, but instead she simply swiped the knife over the edge of the bed onto the floor.

Then she giggled. "Outa sight's outa mind, like mama always said."

"Well, c'mon, man," she added impatiently, resuming her tugging at his trousers. "Help me get your damn pants off."

Duke decided to just get it over with. His dick now felt like it would explode if he didn't relieve the pressure in his balls.

One thing that Duke always appreciated about Katrina was that she gave fantastic head. In less than a minute, she had him squirming all over the bed while she sucked on him, her lips and tongue playing over his penis like fingers handling a saxophone.

Oh, oh, oh, my God! Oh fuck!

She stopped sucking on him for a moment and giggled. "C'mon, honey, return the favor!"

Duke got in position under Katrina, so he could eat her too while she worked on him. Her sex smelt quite pissy, but he was too far gone in his world of pleasure to do anything but taste it.

It's odd, he thought in amusement, *once you are in bed with a woman, you simply dive in and hope for the best.*

She had large pussy lips. He spread those fat labia and licked at the pink tissue in between. She was wet, her sex dripping into his mouth. She squirmed as he tongued her; squirmed and groaned and attacked his penis with renewed fervor. Duke was glad he'd drank some beers earlier: they were helping him hold back. He lifted his head up to Katrina's clitoris and sucked on it. At that, she pulled her mouth off his erection and gasped. Then she flopped sideways off him.

"Put it in me, quick!"

Vague warnings to use a condom flashed through Duke's mind (he didn't have any, and neither did she; this was unwise . . . what if it was that time of month for her?), but Katrina was already pulling him onto her, grabbing hold of his turgid rod and slipping it inside her wetness. Her loins engulfed him; he gasped with satisfaction. He stared down at her. Her emerald eyes were moist, like she'd just gotten through crying.

Oh, God, how beautiful she is!

He bent and kissed her. She responded passionately. Leaning over her with his arms straight, he began thrusting with abandon.

At that moment, a gust of wind blew the curtains away from the window. As the air chilled Duke's back, he glanced at the window, and as his gaze shifted back towards Katrina, he noticed something odd:

The knife. How'd it get up on the bed again? Katrina knocked it onto the floor, I saw her do so.

And now there was another weapon in the room. This one was an axe. It sat on the nightstand. The axe was stained with drops of crusty blood.

Then, about to panic, Duke blinked and everything was normal again; there was neither axe nor knife in sight.

Seeing things or not, his penis was still hard, still dipped in Katrina's tight wetness. He'd kept on thrusting while his attention was diverted from her to the window and back again.

Now he focused on her. She pulled him down onto her, kissed him and ground her breasts against his chest.

"Tell me when you're gonna come, O.K.?" she told him. "I want your come in my mouth." She looked hard at him to emphasize this.

Her voice sounded unfamiliar to him now. Yes, this was Katrina's voice, and yet somehow it wasn't her voice.

Still, he nodded and gasped, "Sure, won't be long now. You're so damn hot, baby. But I don't want to come before you."

Katrina locked her legs around his buttocks. "Don't worry about that. O.K.?"

He gasped a reply and thrust harder.

One, two, three . . .

"Okay, I'm gonna come, I can feel it . . ."

When Duke said this, he expected Katrina to unlock her legs from his ass, but she didn't. He decided that by 'mouth' she'd meant her 'lower mouth.'

"Oh, God, yes, I'm fucking coming," he growled like a hurt animal.

And she was staring up at him with those hypnotic green eyes of hers, and the orgasm was fantastic, one of the best ever, the semen just spurting out of him, and then . . .

And then, Katrina's head suddenly vanished from between her shoulders.

Duke froze in mid-thrust there in the motel room bed. He hung there over Katrina's body, his arms straightened out, staring at the red hole between her shoulders where her head had been just now. The hole wasn't bleeding, it was circular and had a wrinkled, ridged rim. It looked a lot like a massive anus, like feces would shortly pump out of it.

Duke was horrified.

But he was still ejaculating into Katrina, his come spurting deliciously. The sensation locked him in place like he'd been nailed atop her.

It occurred to Duke that he was experiencing yet another insane hyperrealistic dream.

But then, Duke realized that something was sucking him between the legs. Doubly horrified and confused now, he stared down between their bodies.

Oh, shit! What . . .!?

Katrina's missing head was now down between her legs. Her mouth was wrapped around his penis and was sucking hard on it. Sucking his ejaculate deep into her throat.

Only, her throat was where?

The head between Katrina's legs paused in fellating Duke for a moment and twisted sideways to wink up at him.

That wink unfroze Duke. All of his crystalized terrors, everything he'd ever been scared of in his life and had locked away in his subconscious, came to a focus at that moment in time.

Because the face between Katrina's legs wasn't hers; it belonged to Phoenix Aurora, the evil monstrous woman that he'd just gotten through convincing himself was merely a figment of his imagination.

Duke instantly backed off of her. Her feet had since unhooked from his ass, her legs fallen to his sides, so that detaching from her was as easy as pulling out.

Only, he found that he *couldn't* pull out. As he leapt off the headless woman and backed away from the bed, her head came with him, her lips still clamped on his penis (which horribly, was still hard from how tight her mouth was around him, like her lips were a cock-ring slowing the exit of blood from his member.).

He couldn't believe what was happening: Phoenix Aurora's neck was unreeling from between her legs, from her vagina. He could fucking see it! He watched it emerge like a pink snake sliding from its burrow, seemingly endlessly.

Her body lay in bed, her fingers squeezing her nipples, while her neck unreeled after his fleeing form.

No matter how far he went (and it seemed he traveled a thousand miles in the confines of that little room), Duke couldn't get away. Her mouth was stuck in his crotch, her lips and teeth tight on his stiff penis.

He looked down at her. Phoenix Aurora winked at him with eyes the shade of midnight.

He began hitting her, beating the head about the ears and face, sticking his fingers in her nose and pulling back on it; all in an effort to get her off of his penis. Instead though, she bit down harder, her teeth penetrating his skin now. But she clearly wasn't trying to emasculate him, just keeping herself firmly in place on him.

A thin layer of blood squirted from between her lips. Once he saw the blood, he stopped hitting her head and grabbed her long neck instead.

He looked around for his gun, but the trusty Glock was now nowhere in sight.

But all hope wasn't exactly lost. Duke suddenly sighted Phoenix's knife on the floor by the bed. All he had to do was get across to the knife and threaten her with it. She'd let go of him for sure then, and if she didn't . . .

But if I cut her head off, how the hell do I explain it to the cops afterwards? But maybe she'll vanish after she dies!

But, oh God!—the pain between his legs with her teeth dug into him like that! He *had* to get her off his cock.

Then he discovered he was stuck. Stuck to the wall, so that it hurt to try to get away from it.

What? Looking back, Duke saw that the wall had altered. It now looked like skin, like *his* skin stretched left and right to the corners of the room. When he tried stepping forward, he felt his skin stretch, and in addition felt intense agony like it was being peeled off of his body.

Shit!

He was connected—glued, stuck to the wall like a bug in a roach motel, all the way down the rear of his naked body. He made the mistake of attempting to feel the skin on the wall, with the effect that both of his arms also ended up glued in place. Next, he found his head was stuck too . . . and then his thighs and the backs of his calves.

And now that he couldn't move, Phoenix Aurora finally slurped off of his penis.

Wobbling on the super-long neck projecting from between her legs, her head floated around his. She had a black eye from all the hitting he'd done on her.

"So, it wasn't a dream," he complained to her. "All of that stuff over at the Hell House really happened."

"No, it wasn't a dream." She was laughing in satisfaction at his horror. "I really did kill your girlfriend Katrina."

By stretching the wall/body skin of his scalp to an agonizing degree, Duke was able to bend his head forward enough to see his penis. It was just softening, with a bleeding ridged furrow left by Phoenix Aurora's teeth across its upper surface near the root.

He let his head go. Pulled by skin taut as rubber, it flipped back up to smack against the wall again, giving him a headache.

Phoenix Aurora's floating head regarded him in amusement. "I wasn't gonna bite it off, anyway. I'm not that kind of woman."

That said, on the bed she reached down between her legs and pulled her the lips of her vagina apart. She stretched them wide, so that her sex yawned open like a toothless monster mouth (like the maw of the tentacled blob that had killed Katrina), with the emerging rope of neck as its tongue.

Then, winking at Duke, she began her retreat into her hole.

Duke, stuck to the wall—now, in fact, part of the wall—gaped in disbelief as Phoenix Aurora's neck reeled back into her vagina and her head followed after it and slurped away out of sight into her body.

A moment later, her head popped out between her shoulders again.

She reached up and wiped a trail of Duke's semen off her lips, and then licked the finger clean.

"That was a great blowjob, wasn't it?" she asked.

And Duke Higgins, now impossibly part of his own motel room, could only gape and wonder what in the world the evil housekeeper had in store for him next.

CHAPTER 41

Duke . . . Deconstructed

It was very bad.

Duke had a vision of a world where lots of people—men, women, and children—were stuck to walls like he was (their skin now parts of immense flesh buildings), and were suffering all sorts of horrendous torments. Their tormentors were tall and thin blue-skinned demons, humanlike to a degree, but noseless and each having four arms that ended in huge hands with sharp black claws.

And then he woke up.

I slept off? How the fuck could I possibly have slept off? Or have I simply been having another nightmare? Was everything just another bad dream?

His eyes focused. No, it wasn't a dream: Phoenix Aurora was stroking his face.

"C'mon, wakey up," she was cooing.

Duke's eyes focused on her. She stood before him weighing the knife in her hands. And now Duke realized that she'd gagged him. With . . . his socks? The strong smell of sweaty feet filled his nostrils.

She patted his cheek. "C'mon, Duke, wakey up. She-it, this always happens. O.K., nod if I'm right: You just saw that other place, didn't you?"

Forgetting the limitation on motion that being a part of the wall imposed on him, he nodded, then tried to scream as his scalp stretched taut again, feeling like it was being sliced off his head.

She nodded back. "It's a real horrible place. Once upon a time, I was trapped there too, being tormented by the demons, but I escaped, see?"

Duke just stared at the knife in her hands. Phoenix Aurora was holding it up between her perfect breasts, their creamy white flesh beaded with sweat, their nipples erected like she was still sexually charged up.

The silver weapon reflected Duke's bound form back at him. When she turned it slightly, he caught sight of the wall he was now part of. The wall was all hairy and bits of it twitched.

Tough as he was, Duke was terrified.

I really can't be sane and wide awake! This is even crazier than what happened to Katrina!

The opposite wall—the one behind Phoenix Aurora—was normal enough, pale yellow wallpaper and a framed picture of Barbara Streisand . . . Everything else in the room was normal, except for that bloody axe on the bed to his right.

So, no, he hadn't imagined the axe being there during the sex.

Phoenix Aurora giggled. "No, I'm lying, I didn't escape; you can never escape from that damn place, see? It's linked to the house, and the house never lets anyone go. I'm an agent of the house. There are a few others like myself. We have special powers. We can walk thru walls and change shape and things like that . . . As long as I feed the house I can remain here. Do you understand?"

While Duke was trying to understand, Phoenix Aurora stepped up close to him and flashed her knife across his face.

Duke immediately felt a white-hot searing of pain in the middle of his face. The pain didn't cease, it burnt hotter and hotter.

He screamed behind his gag, then gaped at Phoenix Aurora in disbelief.

She was holding his nose up in front of him, red and messy, and air was rushing unhampered into his head, making him all giddy, and his eyes seemed to be crossing.

She grinned, her face splattered red with his blood now.

"The house is hungry, and I must feed it your agony," she told Duke. "Sometimes it wants flesh and blood, but now it wants your pain."

She flung his severed nose away over her shoulder, then bent forward and kissed the bleeding gap where his nose had been.

Then she leaned back and rolled her eyes. "Sorry, Duke, but this is gonna be like really bad sex—it'll take forever to end, and you'll hate it."

Then she grabbed his left ear and began slicing it off.

Duke fainted from the pain; but he was instantly back in the realm with the people being tortured on walls. He too was stuck on a wall there, with one of the blue-skinned demon-folk sticking a burning poker into his guts. Screaming, he fainted there too, and woke up back in the motel room again.

And here and now, Phoenix Aurora was busy slicing off his right ear. And he screamed and screamed in silence behind his gag. And when she finished slicing off his ear, she grabbed his hair and began scalping him. And as she slowly ripped the skin off his skull, Duke blacked out again and flipped across to the other side, but over there the four-armed demon was now plucking out both of his eyes at once, so he woke up again in the motel room, where Phoenix Aurora was now gutting him, pulling his intestines out of his belly.

She was covered in his blood.

Kneeling between his legs, she dragged his guts out in fistfuls, and he kept up his muffled screaming, and he had no idea how this could hurt so much, or why he'd not yet bled to death (she was that blood-splattered), and yet his pain went on and on and on.

And, then, when Phoenix Aurora had yanked all of his guts out (while all the while blinking her dazzling midnight eyes at him; eyes that were the only part of her head that weren't all red with his blood), he thought it would all be over.

His mind a fever of torment, Duke prayed for death now, prayed for it with all of his might.

Heaven or Hell, it didn't matter where he was ending up. What did matter was that this impossible agony stop right now.

He'd not flipped over to the other side again, so maybe he'd already died there.

So fucking let me die here too! God, please, help me die!

But now, disbelieving, Duke watched Phoenix Aurora traipse over to the axe on the bed and pick it up. Then she danced back over to him and raised it. Blood—his blood—was liberally dripping off her face now, red streams dribbling off the ends of her black hair.

"Now, I'm going to hack all of the flesh off of your bones," she enthused. "It's also going to seem to last forever, and it's going to hurt you even more than the earlier torment did."

She began hacking at him. Duke watched dripping wet chunks of his body fly off behind her like red birds.

At some point, he felt the pain begin to fade, and he was pleased when he knew that he was finally dying for good, never to wake again into this horror, or the other one.

But Phoenix Aurora had one last treat of pain in store for the house.

Just before Duke died, she pulled off his gag and slowly sliced both of his lips off his face.

So, Duke died in fantastic agony.

Then Phoenix Aurora kissed his lipless mouth.

CHAPTER 42

Inside Hell House

When Aaron returned with the wheeled makeup case, he found a heated debate being held in the living room.

"I think she was a ghost," Rosa was saying. "How else did she go missing like that?"

"I don't believe she's a ghost," Bobbi replied. "But maybe she's a witch, like Erin De Mornay."

"No, I insist that she's a ghost."

"You're missing the evidence right before your eyes," Erica said.

"And what's that!?" Rosa asked, puffing herself up somewhat in a pose that Aaron was certain she'd been taught at the police academy as the right way to stare criminals down.

"Her name," Erica pointed out. "I don't think her parents named her Phoenix Aurora. She's got a witch's name. Just like that tattoo you've got as a tramp stamp." Her brow creased up when she tried to remember. "What's her name again? Lily Nightshade?"

"Lilith Nightfall," Rosa told her testily. "And she's not a witch, she's a fictional vampire character."

"Whatever. The principle is the same. No one in their right mind ever names their child something like that, except if they worship the devil themselves."

"She's got a point," Tom agreed with a raised finger.

"I still say she's a ghost."

"Stop trying to frighten her," Cedric told Rosa.

"Yeah, just stop already," Erica said.

"I'm not frightened," Bobbi retorted. "I'm just frustrated that Rosa *insists* that a solid person could possibly be unalive."

Tom laughed. "Anyway, there's no point even arguing about this. The lady said she'll be back soon. Once she gets back here, we can ask her which she is: witch or ghost or vampire or werewolf or just plain old small-town psycho bitch."

Erica rolled her eyes at him. "You're worse than Rosa."

The argument sort of fizzled out when they noticed Aaron.

Aaron rolled the makeup case into the living room and then gestured to Erica, who was seated on the arm of the chair that Tom was sitting in.

"Where do you guys want this?" he asked her.

She waved back. "Over there, by the bookcase."

But Bobbi walked over to him and pointed across the living room at a wood-and-metal spiral staircase that connected the floors.

"Actually, it's going upstairs," she told him. "According to our vanished housekeeper, the upper bedrooms are best for us girls."

"Hey, the lady isn't *vanished*," Tom said and began laughing. "Ms. Phoenix Aurora just walked off while we were all preoccupied with trying to see the boner that Rosa gave Cedric by fiddling in his pants."

Everyone laughed.

"Guys, guys, let it go," Cedric pleaded. Cedric looked like he was blushing beneath his dark skin.

"But what if you need the case downstairs tomorrow for your photoshoot?" Aaron asked Bobbi in a low voice. "Do I have to carry it downstairs again?"

Bobbi shrugged. "Maybe, maybe not. We can always do our makeup in our room."

Aaron nodded and then looked around at everyone. "So why aren't we checking out the rooms?" he asked.

"You and me will be rooming downstairs, bro," Tom told him. "I mean, the housekeeper said there's two bedrooms upstairs and two downstairs, so I'm thinking we'll let Bobbi and Erica have one of those and Rosa and Cedric can share the other one."

"That's cool with me," Aaron agreed. "I'll just roll this makeup box upstairs then."

He was about to head for the spiral staircase, but then he noticed something odd about Bobbi, so he stopped and frowned at her.

"Bobbi," he said, "what did you do to your necklace?"

"What do you mean?" she asked him, but then she looked down at the pendant. "Huh!?" she gasped.

The weird black pendant had begun glowing again. Its glow was faint, just barely perceptible, like a light bulb accessing a very low voltage. But as she and Aaron watched, it began glowing brighter.

Bobbi turned to look at the others. "Hey, guys, it's started up again."

"What's started up again?" Erica asked, but then her gaze followed Bobbi's pointing finger, which was jabbing towards her chest like a knife uncertain if it wanted to stab her in the heart or not.

And now, with everyone's attention focused on Bobbi, the pendant began strongly strobing the living room in its creepy negative light.

"I feel like a walking discotheque," Bobbi complained. "What the fuck?" She plucked the pendant up off her chest and studied it in confusion.

"When did it resume doing that?" Erica asked.

"I don't know; I only just noticed."

Erica and the others got to their feet and gathered around Aaron and Bobbi.

"This is weird," Tom said, leaning forward and peering down at the pendant that Bobbi clutched in her trembling fingers. He turned to Aaron. "Bro, what do you make of this?"

"I might be wrong about this," Aaron said cautiously, "but judging from what Phoenix Aurora said, I think it began pulsing again the moment Bobbi walked into the house. Maybe at first it was collecting energy and pulsing very subtly, but now it's properly linked up with the house and—"

His explanation was cut short when the pendant flung out a massive burst of black light that seemed to fill the living room.

Startled by this, Bobbi instantly let go of the pendant, so that it once more dropped between her breasts.

For the duration that the reversed illumination lasted, Aaron saw everyone in the room as black and white images—he could clearly see everyone's skeletons glowing white inside of their black flesh.

And then Aaron clearly saw the dark illumination 'reverse and repack itself' (this was the only description that accurately described what he was witnessing) back into the pendant.

The flash of light ended. Monochrome became normal chromatic light. The everyday color scheme once more prevailed.

"What the fuck?" everyone present *silently* asked in unison.

"Is it gonna continue doing this?" Erica asked Bobbi next. " 'Cos if it is, I suggest you take it off and carry it in your purse instead."

"Yeah, this stuff is freaky," Cedric agreed with a worried expression on his face. "Just now, I thought I could see the bones in each of our bodies."

"Me as well, bro," Tom added, with Erica and Rosa nodding their agreement.

"It didn't do this earlier, when we were outside by our rides," Rosa said.

"No, it didn't," Tom agreed. "I wonder why it's doing so now?"

But Aaron wasn't sure that it hadn't. All of a sudden, he seemed to recollect a strange dream that he'd had a short while ago, but while he'd still been awake, in which exactly the same x-ray effect had occurred.

So, it might have happened—our insides might've appeared transparent back when were outside near the cars—only, none of us noticed it . . . or can remember it . . .

"I'll take it off," Bobbi agreed. "At least until Phoenix Aurora comes back and explains how it works and what it does."

But then she yelped loudly.

No one present needed to ask what had just startled Bobbi. They'd noticed what she had.

Where previously, they'd each been too shocked by the pendant's weird explosion of light to pay proper attention to the change in it, now everyone saw that Bobbi's necklace had at some recent point in time tightened itself around her neck. Now it hugged her throat like a choker.

"How the heck did it do that?" Tom asked.

"*When* did it shorten up like that?" Rosa asked.

"Does it hurt?" Erica asked.

"No, it doesn't hurt," Bobbi replied. "It's just tight enough to not be uncomfortable."

"Turn around and I'll untie the knot at the back," Aaron told Bobbi. "We can get it off that way."

"I'll do it." Rosa, who was standing behind Bobbi, was already parting her hair at the back for a look.

Then Rosa paused and looked around at everyone in surprise. "Guys, it doesn't have a knot anymore," she told them all.

"What?" everyone gasped.

But it was true. When Aaron got Bobbi turned around and examined the rear of her necklace, he saw that the knot previously tied in the cords had vanished and that both ends of said cords were now seamlessly fused together behind Bobbi's neck, as if they'd been that way from the very beginning.

Meaning that now, the only way to get the necklace off of her would be to cut it off, a course of action that Aaron very much doubted Bobbi Kolinski would ever agree to.

"I guess the housekeeper was right about the necklace knowing that it's back home," Tom said.

Erica nudged him with her elbow. "Don't say that. Consider Bobbi's feelings."

But Bobbi shook her head. "Don't worry, I feel fine. It's like something just erased my worries."

"Well, that's good then," Aaron said cautiously. "We can all wait for the housekeeper to return and explain to us how we can get the necklace off of Bobbi."

"But I don't wanna take it off anymore," Bobbi protested, with a somewhat dreamy smile on her face.

Aaron nodded. "Whatever you say. But in the meantime, guys, let's get ourselves settled in our rooms."

"Hey, I thought Billy and his friends just stepped out for a walk," Cedric said. "Shouldn't they have come back by now?"

"And we *still* don't have any cell service," Rosa pointed out, flinging her hands up in exasperation. "Life on Earth could have ended out there and we wouldn't know."

"C'mon, guys," Aaron said a little nervously, "let's not get started digging up that rabbit hole again. We know for certain that Billy and his friends are over at McDonald's eating burgers. So, let's get ourselves settled in, huh?"

"We're on the downstairs, bro," Tom said and picked up his bags.

To Aaron's relief, the others followed suit. Everyone picked up their bags and stuff and prepared to disperse from the living room.

"Hey, guys," Rosa said loudly just as they were about splitting up.

Everyone gave her their attention.

"What's the matter, baby?" Cedric asked, once more laden down with both his stuff and hers.

Rosa sighed and said, "Okay, now I don't like to be a creepy bitch and point this out, but this is how just about every horror movie I've seen begins: You know, four or five friends arrive at a creepy location and meet a creepy person and—" she wagged her cellphone at the others, "—and suddenly there's no phone service . . . and then creepy shit starts to happen to them." She sighed again. "Oh yeah, and then they all get killed and eaten by the monsters."

To Be Continued . . .

ABOUT THE AUTHOR

Wol-vriey is Nigerian, and quite tall.

He believes there actually are things that go bump in the night.

He writes horror fiction—for adults only, please. And also some surrealist stuff.

Wol-vriey blogs at: *http://oddityfarm.wordpress.com*

WOL-VRIEY
BIZARRO AND TRANSGRESSIVE FICTION

BOSTON POSH (BUD MALONE #1)

In 2028 AD, the USA is a nation ravaged by hungry dragons and dinosaurs. In Boston, Massachusetts, private eye Bud Malone is hired to rescue a kidnapped heiress. But nothing is as it seems.

Malone works to unravel a tangled web involving Boston Chinatown, a 200-year-old woman with a 9-year-old body, white robots, a human-liver-eating psychopath, a golem, a porcelain dragon, and a snake goddess with a crush on him. There's also a woman obsessed with chicken sex. Then Malone meets Posh Lane, a gorgeous call girl who's desperate to quit her pimp.

Romantic sparks ignite between Posh and Malone, but Posh's past suddenly catches up with her in a BIG way. To save Posh, Malone agrees to run a quest for Earth's new rulers, the Forks. But, Malone has no idea that agreeing to the Fork's odd request will send him on the weirdest trip he's ever been on in his life.

BOSTON CORPSE (BUD MALONE #2)

MAGIC CAN BE MURDER! - Drag queen Lucy Tang is back in Boston, and is hell-bent on settling her vindetta against casino owner Sookie Ling. And suddenly, Bud Malone, PI, has the case of his life to resolve.

When Boston's robot police force are baffled by a mind transfer case, they come to Malone for help. The one person who can likely help Malone out here is the witch Soledad Bathory. But Soledad seems to know a lot more than she's telling him. It's a case not made easier when Malone meets Soledad's beautiful cousin, Josephine 'Slave' Bailey. Slave has her own plans for Malone, most of which involve teaching him BDSM and making him her new Master.

Oh, and Rick Rogers owes Sookie Ling a whole lot of money, a gambling debt that's going to be literally Hell to pay!

BOSTON CORPSE - Not your average detective novel!

Burning Bulb

WOL-VRIEY
BIZARRO AND TRANSGRESSIVE FICTION

BOSTON LUST (BUD MALONE #3)

"Bless it, Father, for she has sinned."

Seven murdered gay women, all their bodies completely drained of blood. All also with large parts of their bodies dissolved away like acid has been pumped into their veins.

Bud Malone has to find the female vampire preying on Boston's lesbian population.

Then Malone meets the beautiful Trudi Carmen and the case gets even more tangled. Trudi needs Malone's help in recovering a ring that's gone missing. But how in the world is one little black ring related to either the dead women or their killer?

Resolving this case will lead Malone deep into Lucy Tang's legacy—the Abstracta. And then to the city of Genesis.

Boston Lust—Just when you thought Bean Town was safe to visit again.

HELL DANCER

Six people find themselves trapped in Detention, a nightmare realm where the demonic Schoolmaster is hell-bent on reforming them . . . until they die.

Porn superstar Venus Deluxe came to Springfield, MA to party, and next found her life hanging by a thread. One wrong answer will mean her death.

Suspended BPD detective Tanya Rockford was trying to stop one kind of violence, but found a terrifying another. With her and her companion's lives hanging in the balance, it's going to take all of her courage and resourcefulness to escape this hell she's stumbled into.

Porn stud Chad Cannon has made a career from his ten-inch penis. Here in Detention, however, it's his brains that matter. He'll soon be hoping all the pot he's smoked over the years hasn't completely messed up his memory.

The three students, Sherri, Jordan, and Mike? They were all just in the wrong place at the right time. Will anyone survive Detention? The evil Schoolmaster doesn't plan on letting that happen . . .

WOL-VRIEY
BIZARRO AND TRANSGRESSIVE FICTION

VAGINA MUNDI

Rachel Risk is a professional thief with super-strong hair that can stretch like tentacles to manipulate objects. Ashley Status has both a digitally augmented brain, and 'muscle-purses' in her arms and legs in which she stores inflatable objects—cars, guns, rocket launchers, etc.

When Raye is framed as the fall girl in a jewel robbery, the pair flee Chicago's vengeful robot gangsters and take refuge in the Hotel Bizarre, where the gorgeous 'vagina singer,' Femina, is performing for a week.

But the Hotel Bizarre is even stranger than its name suggests, and very soon Raye and Ash are involved in an deadly adventure, a struggle for survival the likes of which they'd never imagined possible with loads of deviant sex, drugs, music, and violence at every turn. And just what is the old woman in the skin desert really doing with all those cats glued to her walls?

VAGINA MUNDI—a Bizarro Hymn in praise of WOMAN!

VEGAN VAMPIRE VAGINAS

The biggest bank heist in US history. And Tom Palmer can't remember pulling it off. And no, this isn't your standard case of amnesia. After a one-night-stand gone horribly wrong, Boston salesman Tom Palmer wakes up with a vagina implanted in his left hand. Then his day gets worse.

Tom is transported across space-time to a nightmare version of Boston, one where the Bizarro virus has transformed half the population into cannibals. Worst of all, Tom discovers that in this new Boston, he's the infamous gangster Pussypalm, wanted for robbing the Federal Reserve Bank of Boston a year ago. He also learns that the vagina in his hand is prophetic, i.e. it talks . . . after sex.

With 130 people left dead during his bank heist and six billion dollars missing, Tom knows he's living on borrowed time. It is in his best interests not to remember anything. Because once he does . .

Burning Bulb

WOL-VRIEY

BIZARRO AND TRANSGRESSIVE FICTION

VEGAN ZOMBIE APOCALYPSE

In the post-apocalypse worlderness, zombies rule the earth. They're allergic to meat, and brains literally make them explode. Zombies now eat blood potatoes, parasitic tubers grown in the flesh of humancows corralled in maximum security farms. Two fugitives meet in the ancient ruins of Texas. The first is Soil 15-f, a womancow who's escaped her farm a week before she's due to be killed and her blood potato crop harvested. The second fugitive is Able Kane, former head necros food technician, now sentenced to death for heresy. But Soil is no ordinary humancow.

Unknown to herself, she's the vegan zombie agricultural revolution, and the zombies desperately want her back. And the necros equally desperately want Able Kane dead. He's fled with a forbidden discovery which will reshape the world for the worse if used. And Able is just hardheaded/misguided enough to use it.

MELANIE NEMESIS CATCHPOLE

In Springfield, Massachusetts, Melanie Catchpole is hired to fetch back a magic teddy bear worth millions of dollars from a warehouse across town. Problem is, the warehouse is down in Springfield's O-Zone that totally weird sector of the city where Bizarro fell to Earth. The 'O' is a fairytale land, a place where dreams and nightmares literally live and breathe..

Worse still, the gingers—mutant cannibals—prowl the O. The gingers have already eaten everyone else Melanie's employers sent to get back the magic teddy bear.

Accompanied by the handsome but ruthless Doug Fisher (who she finds sexy but doesn't dare entrust her heart to), Melanie enters the O-Zone. Melanie and Doug are instantly caught up in an adventure they'd never have believed credible even if written as fiction . . . and Melanie's used to experiencing the very weird as the norm.

And now, additionally, there's a mystery to unravel: What does the dark, freezing-cold being called The Fixer want with Mary, the barkeep's daughter?

Burning Bulb

WOL-VRIEY
BIZARRO AND TRANSGRESSIVE FICTION

BIG TROUBLE IN LITTLE ASS

From Bizarro master storyteller Wol-vriey comes a truly weird western tale that will leave you awe-struck and on the edge of your seat...

In the town named Little Ass, tight-assed prostitute Rosa overhears a gunslinger's plans to assassinate rancher Edison Bennett. Once the badass Bennett learns of the plot, he ensures there'll be hell to pay for any attempt on his life!

Yes, it's going to take all of gunslinger Jude's shooting prowess, his eclectic collection of strange firearms, a trusty horse that requires an owners' manual, and the help of the lovely and invigorating Nell (who's EXTREMELY odd when the going gets weird), to survive the Bizarro hell that Edison Bennett unleashes in order to hold onto the land that he'd stolen from Madam Zizi.

BIZARRO 101 (A BASIC PRIMER)

Welcome to the strange place:

A collection of 37 flash fiction stories designed to introduce one to the Bizarro/New Weird Genre.

Weird, dreamy, nightmarish, absurd, sad, surreal, humorous . . . this collection of tales is all this and more.

***

"This primer is the very essence of any and all styles and types of Bizarro writing. Wol-vriey collects, distills, and bottles up these 37 tiny stories for your sensory enjoyment. This is an absolute must-read for anyone new to the genre, because it demonstrates the scope of what Bizarro is, and what it can be."
— Teresa Pollack, Bizarro commentator and blogger

Burning Bulb

WOL-VRIEY
BIZARRO AND TRANSGRESSIVE FICTION

Dr. Orgasm

Courtney Taylor is young, intelligent, beautiful, and successful. She also has a boyfriend who loves her deeply. The problem is, no matter what Courtney does, she can't climax during sex.

When Florence Rigid's communist forces destroy the city of Metaphor, Courtney and her friends Teresa, Highball, Miki, and Heather are cast into the midst of a quest to find the only person able to save the land of Innuendo—Dr. Carol Orgasm, wanted by the communists for developing the O-Pill, a wonder drug that grants women sexual ecstasy on demand.

The communists will do anything to get their hands on the O-Pill and prevent its reaching the millions of Innuendo's women. But Courtney desperately wants that pill too. And so it's now a race between Courtney and the communists to find Dr. Orgasm first.

And Courtney has no choice but to win this race. She must win it: For her own orgasm . . . and for the freedom of female sexuality everywhere.

PUSSY TRANSMISSION

Pussy Transmission were the most decadent Pop Art ensemble of the 90's. Led by the beautiful painter Isis Lynch, the trio revolutionized the art world. Then suddenly, without explanation, Pussy Transmission vanished into historical obscurity. Now, twenty years later, three women come to Lynch Place. Lily and Nina are journalists desperate to interview Isis Lynch. Raven, on the other hand, wants to find her boyfriend, who's gone missing inside Isis's house. Raven's worried—she's heard that Pussy Transmission broke up because Isis began dabbling in black magic . . . with devastating results. All three women will shortly wish they'd never left home. Particularly once the rats in Lynch Place start warning them that they're going to die . . . and Raven meets Betty Butcher, the bouncy supernatural psycho who's intent on chopping her into bits. Pussy Transmission, Baby! Just because . . .

Burning Bulb

WOL-VRIEY
BIZARRO AND TRANSGRESSIVE FICTION

GIRLS ARE NOT SMILING

Welcome To The Road Trip From Hell

Pagan is demon-possessed.

Lori is suicidal.

Britt is just terminally pissed off.

Meet three young Boston women on the run from the law, each with problems that will fuse into more than the sum of their individual parts, becoming a holocaust of sex and violence and terror, a literal rain of blood and horror and gore and evil.

And if that wasn't already bad enough, Pagan's pet demon is slowly transforming her into something both unspeakable and unholy. Truly, these girls aren't smiling.

BLUE NIGHTMARES

Consummate EVIL is coming.   It is relentless and unavoidable. It is Blue.

Jessica Schreiber is seeing things. Very horrible things. Since arriving in Raynham for what should have been a relaxing vacation, she's been seeing *The Big Blue*.

Jessica is smelling things too—dead and rotting things that she can't see. She is sure those dead and rotting things are dead people. Lots of dead people.

Jessica's worst nightmares will soon become her reality. Her reality will soon become a terrifying nightmare.

The tentacled residents of the House of Death have a lot that they wish to show Jessica Schreiber. They have a lot that they wish to tell her. But will she survive long enough to learn their lessons?

Burning Bulb

WOL-VRIEY
BIZARRO AND TRANSGRESSIVE FICTION

BRAINCHEW

It was supposed to be a simple jewel heist, but it went badly wrong. Chuck got shot and died.

Lance hid his friend's corpse in the Pleasant Street Cemetery. But that was a big mistake—there was something undead, something extremely hungry . . . something eXXXtremely horrible, buried in the Pleasant Street Cemetery.

And Lance had just woken it up.

They called the monster Brainchew because it ate brains. Human brains. And it preferred those brains fresh from the heads . . . of the living.

And now it was awake again, Brainchew planned on feeding big-time tonight. Oh hell yes, it did.

BRAINCHEW 2: OUT OF THEIR HEADS

After Tiff Hooper recognizes Josh Penham, the man who abducted her and kept her in his basement and abused her, she brings her three friends to Raynham for a night of well-deserved revenge on him.

Only things don't go according to plan.

It is never a good idea to leave a corpse in Raynham's Pleasant Street Cemetery. You run the very real risk of awakening what lies underground there. And that thing—Brainchew—is more horrible and more evil than anything the average mind conceives of even in its worst nightmares.

Brainchew is back! And this time the monster is extra-hungry. But there are plenty of delicious human brains about tonight, and Brainchew intends to eat them all before dawn.

Burning Bulb

WOL-VRIEY
BIZARRO AND TRANSGRESSIVE FICTION

DARIA: AN EROTIC NIGHTMARE

Even the best laid women can go wrong.

Daria Simpson is HUNGRY. She's HUNGRY for sex and bloodshed and death.

Shelly Parker just wanted to have a threesome with her boyfriend Craig and her best friend Erica. Everything was shaping up nicely for their weekend of sexual fun and games, until they stopped at the creepy Crossway Diner and met Daria.

From the moment they met Daria, EVERYTHING went wrong for them; and it went wrong in the most horrific and terrifying of ways!

Daria: Paranormal service has been resumed.

WET BONES

Greg is about learning the hard way that you don't mess with Aunt Grace.

Nine completely fleshless skeletons recovered in the Massachusetts woods. Two detectives on the trail of a horrible, hungry monster.

Broken-hearted Allie Jackson has a date with a creature from Hell.

Things are about to get well out of hand for everyone, and in horrifying, terrifying ways they don't expect.

Burning Bulb

WOL-VRIEY
BIZARRO AND TRANSGRESSIVE FICTION

MR. UGLY

When a rotting corpse appears and starts butchering Raynham's youths, there's really only one question that needs answering:

Is this faceless and rotting monster Peter Howard, or isn't it?

Problem is, Peter Howard died 15 years ago. So how can he possibly be back from the dead and murdering people with such relentless and incredible brutality?

Peter's mother Malicia, who's just been released from the lunatic asylum may have the answers to the crazy puzzle, but the two detectives investigating the deaths don't even know the right questions to ask her yet.

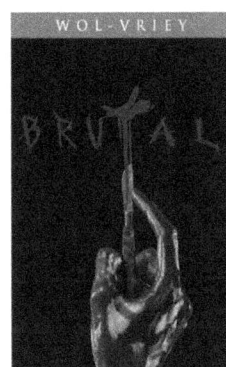

BRUTAL

Jane Winters is 28 years old.

She works as a checkout cashier in a department store. She's an attractive woman with a winning personality. She has both a photographic memory and an I.Q. of 189.

She's met the man of her dreams.

But she's also a cannibal with a unique and very scary mode of operation.

The group known as TULIP (The Urban Legend Investigation People) are out to either prove or disprove the legend of Insane Jane.

But have TULIP bitten off more than they can chew?

Burning Bulb

WOL-VRIEY
BIZARRO AND TRANSGRESSIVE FICTION

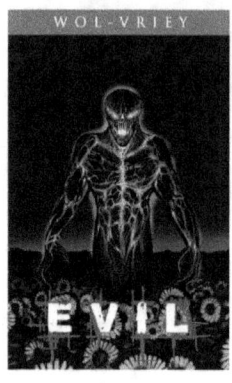

EVIL

The Evil began the week before Sylvia Stewart's 30th birthday.

Cathy Higgins died.

The Bargainer resurrected Cathy . . . for a price.

The price? Cathy's father Ronan had to plant some seeds for him.

But these were no ordinary seeds the Bargainer gave to Ronan Higgins. These were seeds from Hell: seeds which required human flesh as both soil and fertilizer.

And meanwhile, the unsuspecting Sylvia Stewart went ahead with the plans for her birthday party, which was to be held on Ronan Higgins' sunflower farm . . .

666

Ohio's State Route 666 stretches 14.7 miles between Zanesville and Dresden.

Most days, it's just a normal road with a funny name.

But for six minutes on the 6th of June each year, Route 666 becomes a gateway to somewhere else . . . a gateway to Hell.

Each year 13 unfortunates get trapped in the 666 underworld, with no way to get back home.

This year though, things are going to be very different. For one thing, there are currently a whole lot of turbulent human emotions at play in the underworld. And also . . . the psycho Al Gore is just about completing his collection of human heads.

And . . . what the hell is a church doing in Hell, of all places?

Burning Bulb

WOL-VRIEY
BIZARRO AND TRANSGRESSIVE FICTION

THE CLEAVERMAN

It began as a joke, a gag to pass the time that turned deadly. One rainy August night in Raynham, MA, nine friends jokingly invoke the evil phantom butcher called the Cleaverman.

These nine friends get a whole lot more than they ever bargained for. Because there's only one way to return the deadly Cleaverman back to the darkness he came from, and that is to solve his riddle, which starts: "Tell me the name of John Cleaverman's wife . . ."

And human beings being what we are, even with the Cleaverman out to butcher them all, our nine friends still manage to stir A WHOLE LOT of human misbehavior into the deadly mix.

At the rate they're going, it'll be a wonder if anyone survives THE CLEAVERMAN at all.

PERVERSE

When 21-year-old Heather Forrest accompanies three of her friends on a weekend trip up to Vermont, she has no idea what she's getting into.

Because, during a brief stop in the western Massachusetts woods, the girls get kidnapped and things go rapidly downhill from there. Soon Heather and her friends are fighting for their lives, fighting to survive the most perverted and impossible situation imaginable. And meanwhile, Hank Rollins is also in the woods, hunting the unholy monster that killed his wife and son . . . and he's hunting it with live human bait.

Oh yes, there will be blood. And there will be terror and buckets of gore also. And truly horrible atrocities will happen. Most definitely so.

Burning Bulb

WOL-VRIEY
BIZARRO AND TRANSGRESSIVE FICTION

THE VIRGIN

10 million dollars in prize money. 1000+ video cameras, lots of deadly weapons, 10 Suitors, 5 Virgins & 3 Hours . . . to keep your hymen intact.

Hailey Osborne wants to sell her virginity for a hundred thousand dollars. But then she's made an offer she really can't refuse: how about competing to win ten million dollars in a no-holds-barred underground game show, where all she has to do is remain a virgin?

There's just two problems:
1. Four other women also want that prize money.
2. There's ten suitors all contesting to take Hailey and the other virgins' precious hymens . . . by any means necessary . . .

But hey, it's just for 3 hours, right? How hard can it possibly be? Hailey Osborne is about to find out.

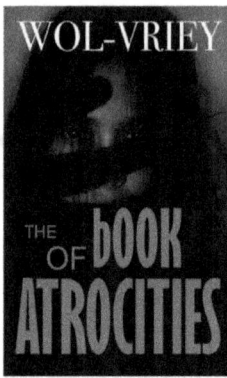

THE BOOK OF ATROCITIES

Bestselling author Drake Melville has been missing for three years now. Drake vanished after publishing The Bleeding Oysters, an epic novel that set new standards for depictions of sleaze and depravity and human monstrosity in popular fiction. On vanishing, however, Drake Melville left a message for everyone, saying he'd 'left town' to go work on his follow-up novel The Book of Atrocities. The problem was, no one could find Drake. It seemed like he'd vanished off the face of the Earth. And now, three years later, Drake has just sent messages to his ex-wife Liz, his current (and abandoned) wife Melody; and his younger sister Chloe . . . asking them to meet him in Raynham, MA. Drake says he's now completed The Book of Atrocities and is ready to present it to the world. But there's a whole lot that Liz, Melody, and Chloe Melville don't know about Drake's Book of Atrocities. And unfortunately they're on their way to find out those excruciatingly painful truths. Because, see, Drake Melville is a VERY EVIL man with a VERY EVIL plan . . .

Burning Bulb

WOL-VRIEY
BIZARRO AND TRANSGRESSIVE FICTION

THE FINAL GIRL

Here there be monsters . . . because we made them.

At a secret location, 8 young women assemble to compete on the ultimate reality/game show—The Final Girl. The 8 contestants are: A young wife and her grown-up stepdaughter, a police detective, a prostitute, a nurse, a school teacher, and unemployed twin sisters.

The Final Girl is a no-holds-barred show beamed to an audience on the Dark Web, a show where murder is permitted and mutilation is encouraged.

The Rules:
1. Avoid being killed and eaten by the show's monsters and bogeymen.
2. Find the prize money—24 million dollars in cash.
3. Hold on to the money.

But only 1 woman can win. And to win The Final Girl reality show, that woman will need to be even more bloodthirsty and ruthless than the show's monsters.

Have a seat, everyone. The most dangerous game is about to begin!

WOMEN

John Miller must die . . . TONIGHT!

Megan Kemp initially went to the Penderson Mansion to collect a debt. But from the moment she stepped in there, getting back outside proved extremely difficult. And then what had merely been difficult for Megan suddenly turned deadly. Because something was going on in the Penderson Mansion that night. Five VERY ANGRY women had a score to settle, and no obstacle on earth would stop them. . . . And no one would get in their way and live to tell the tale either.

"John Miller must die," the women had decreed, and it looked like the forces of Hell would help them accomplish their deadly aim tonight.

But as the night progressed, Megan, who was now trapped in a deadly game of cat and mouse in the Penderson Mansion, found that despite her own troubles, her biggest question was: "What the hell did John Miller do to anger these five women this much?"

Beware, folks . . . sometimes things really do go too far!

Burning Bulb

WOL-VRIEY
BIZARRO AND TRANSGRESSIVE FICTION

RATIO OF BROOKES TO ASHLEYS

After being cursed by a dying woman, Mike Broadman's love life completely nosedives. One girlfriend cheats on him and the next one dies a very messy death.

Next, a psychic informs Mike that he's under an evil spell that will keep killing his girlfriends, and that the ONLY solution (the ONLY way that he'll ever have a happy love life again) is for him to only date women named either Brooke or Ashley from now on.

Mike tries to comply with this, but still, the deaths continue, and now they're becoming even more brutal and bloody. Mike now finds himself in a race against time. He needs to 'equalize the ratio of Brookes to Ashleys' before it's too late.

And then, just when it seems things can't get any crazier or deadlier for Mike, he meets 'Brash' — the twins Brooke and Ashley Lawrence . . .

And the body count keeps rising . . .

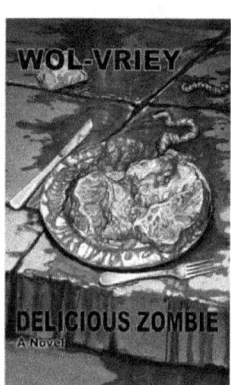

DELICIOUS ZOMBIE

The zombie apocalypse happened two years ago. Today, zombies are mankind's new cattle. The undead are headed like cows and killed and eaten by everyone. The reason for this atrocity? Eating zombie meat has been scientifically proven to reverse human aging. Therefore, anyone who eats the zombies will live forever. Nowadays there are no old people anywhere on Earth. Everyone is young and healthy. Even deadly diseases have regressed. "

Digestion is Salvation," the Church of Zombie preaches. But three people—scientist Ethan Hackman, ex CIA assassin Paula Neyman, and socialite Zoe Patterson—seek to change this madness that is modern life.

With a group of ruthless and sadistic bounty hunters hot on their trail as they attempt to save the world, will Ethan, Paula, and Zoe succeed in curing the zombies, or will the age of the 'Delicious Zombie' continue? One thing is for certain, however; there will be a HUGE amount of murder and mutilation, bloodshed, violence and gore before the knotty issue of the zombies' food status is resolved.

Burning Bulb

WOL-VRIEY
BIZARRO AND TRANSGRESSIVE FICTION

MOTEL GOTHIC

The Devil's Coin Game was a game for desperate men. And Dooks, Hicks, and Robby were three such men, men with nothing to lose, men prepared to gamble their lives away on the flip of a coin. The rules of the game were simple: one man would die, the other two would have their wishes granted by the devil. At midnight in the Sunflower Motel, the Devil's Coin Game will be played, and one of the players will not survive.

Elsewhere in the Sunflower Motel, two female assassins Mandy Cherry and Dewdrop arrive to murder someone. But things are guaranteed to go awry when the intended victim is a witch.

And on this same portentous night, Roman is about to have an unforgettable meeting with a prostitute named Christine. Christine Valona supposedly brings bad luck to all those who encounter her; but why is this, and who is she?

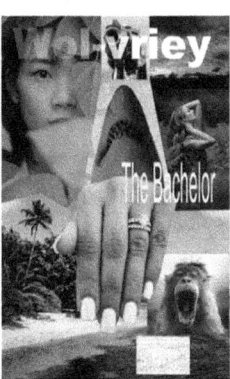

THE BACHELOR

One eligible bachelor, thirteen gorgeous young women, and a TV crew, on a remote Pacific island paradise. What could possibly go wrong? A lot!

Tired of his refusal to get married and make her some grandchildren, American playboy Tyler Bradley is given a 90-day ultimatum by his wealthy mother to either get married or be disowned.

As a solution, Tyler's best friend, TV producer Disney Dizzford suggests that they hold a 'bachelor-seeking-love' themed reality show on Eternity Island, a remote island paradise off of the coast of Guatemala, which for some reason the Guatemalan government pretends doesn't exist. "When the black cloud comes," the strange old man warned, "monsters will emerge from the sea. When the black cloud covers the sky, all will die."

But nobody takes the old guy seriously, because of course this is the 21st century and there are no such things as sea monsters, right? That sort of stuff only happens in bad movies, right?

Wrong. The black cloud just arrived over Eternity Island . . .

Burning Bulb

WOL-VRIEY
BIZARRO AND TRANSGRESSIVE FICTION

MARRIAGE

Adam Norwood, suffering from an extreme photosensitivity skin condition, resides on a secluded island with his wife, Phoebe, and his possible wizard of a father-in-law, Lester. Despite outward appearances of a happy marriage, Adam's life is plagued by recurring nightmares in which Phoebe repeatedly kills him, driving him to the brink of insanity. To add to his woes, Hilary Burton, an alluring party guest on Goat Island, mistakenly identifies Adam as her former lover and is determined to win him back, setting the stage for a calamity that threatens the lives of everyone on the island.

Adam's condition and nightmarish visions pale in comparison to the impending peril he's about to face. The arrival of Hilary Burton unravels a sinister chain of events that may jeopardize the very existence of the island's residents, pushing Adam to discover a new and dire meaning of "bad" and "deadly."

THE MAN WHO KILLED HIS WIFE

Maryanne Wilson's death was definitely an accident. Her husband Bob had absolutely no intention of killing her.

But it was almost certain that a court of law would see things differently, particularly after Bob had sex with Maryanne's corpse . . . and that was why Bob Wilson decided not to call in the police, but to seek an alternative solution to the problem he'd gotten himself into . . . A solution which unfortunately only made matters a whole lot worse for him.

Everything began because Bob Wilson was working too hard and as a result was neglecting his loving wife, Maryanne.

And so, Maryanne asked their upstairs neighbor Jennifer for help.

Jennifer Haskins apparently knew a little magic, and so she cast a spell on Bob, one that would help Maryanne get laid on a more regular basis, like every night if she so desired.

What could possibly go wrong with a simple arrangement like that? Everything you can't possibly imagine . . .

Burning Bulb

WOL-VRIEY
BIZARRO AND TRANSGRESSIVE FICTION

WOL-VRIEY

LGBT: LUST, GORE, BLOODSHED, & TERROR

Hey, you want something completely effed up? Well, here it is! LUST: Lavelle, the lesbian porno actress whose dead lover comes back as a ghost to haunt her. GORE: Greg, the elderly gay man who decides to butcher his young, unfaithful husband and his husband's boyfriend. BLOODSHED: Bryn, the bisexual vampire endlessly seeking her soulmate, but who, somehow, always ends up killing her lovers. TERROR: Tammi, the disgraced transgender influencer who, unable to afford the cost of her Gender Affirmation Surgery, decides to become a 'complete woman' by magical means. These four people meet and interact at the Bonner's Corner nightclub, where their intersecting schemes and dreams will place them on a series of collision courses with each other that will lead to weird consequences for some and horrifying ends for others. Oh, and the witch named Rainbow. Why is Rainbow called 'Rainbow' anyway?

NIGHTMARE FUEL

After Dustin's girlfriend breaks up with him, his new neighbors introduce him to the Real Dreams club to help him get over the breakup. But the Real Dreams club is much stranger than it appears. While on the surface, Real Dreams appears to be a members-only sex club, everything at Real Dreams is fueled by the hallucinogenic drink called Nightmare Fuel, or *Nif* for short. Under *Nif's* strange influence, sex, torture, and murder are merely the tip of an iceberg of depravity, an insane debauched whirlwind that revolves around the worship of the worm goddess Boku Veeza. What exactly has Dustin gotten himself into? Because the longer he remains at the club, the crazier his life becomes. Dustin knows that the Real Dreams club members are keeping a huge secret from him. But can he learn what their secret is and save himself from the unsuspected and unholy terrors of . . . NIGHTMARE FUEL!

Burning Bulb

WOL-VRIEY
BIZARRO AND TRANSGRESSIVE FICTION

NIGHTMARE FUEL 2

Dustin Mitchell thought he was done with the Real Dreams club. He was wrong.

After stopping a brutal murder across the street, Dustin discovers the cult of the worm goddess Boku Veeza is hiding in plain sight. And when a seductive new neighbor moves in, he's pulled into a nightmare of blood, obsession, and dark ritual.

Haunted by visions, hunted by zealots, and lured by the mind-warping drink known as Nightmare Fuel, Dustin must fight to save his sanity—and the woman he loves—from becoming Boku Veeza's next offering.

But the goddess isn't just watching. She wants something.

And she always gets what she wants.

HOW TO SUCCEED IN LIFE

Unlock success... at the cost of your soul.

Grady Burke was delivering a pizza when he found the evil book—or rather, when it found him.

Living with his transgender porn-star sister and mob-connected father, Grady wasn't exactly a slacker, just painfully unmotivated. Maybe that's why the book, titled How to Succeed in Life, chose him.

Soon, people around him start dying in gruesome ways, and Grady must figure out how to survive the book's sinister secrets before it destroys everyone he loves.

How to Succeed in Life: The world's deadliest self-help manual.

Burning Bulb

www.ingramcontent.com/pod-product-compliance
Lightning Source LLC
Chambersburg PA
CBHW070025260626
47159CB00005B/1958